Weary ~~Hearts & Mountain Spirits~~

Hearts at Stake

J. L. Dawson

Weary Hearts and Wounded Spirits

Hearts at Stake

By J L Dawson

Butterfly Books
PUBLISHING

Cover design by: JoAnn Durgin
Edited by: Sharon Dean
ISBN (Paperback) 978-1-7386019-0-5
ISBN (E-book) 978-1-7386018-9-9
A CiP catalogue record for this title is available from the National Library of New Zealand.

First edition, 2024 Butterfly Books Publishing

Contact the author or subscribe to newsletter:
jldawsonauthor@yahoo.com
www.jodawsonauthor.com

Contents

Chapter 1	1
Chapter 2	13
Chapter 3	20
Chapter 4	28
Chapter 5	40
Chapter 6	48
Chapter 7	58
Chapter 8	68
Chapter 9	76
Chapter 10	84
Chapter 11	92
Chapter 12	105
Chapter 13	112
Chapter 14	123
Chapter 15	131
Chapter 16	141
Chapter 17	157
About the Author	162
More books by J. L. Dawson	163

One

Doctor Reynolds looked up at Alice and gave her a compassionate smile. He looked from her face to her twin brother's who sat next to her, gripping her hand. Both faces displayed a mix of apprehension and fear.

"Miss Knight." The doctor closed his eyes and exhaled. His heart ached for what this young woman had faced. He lifted his head. "I'm sorry, it's as you feared. You are indeed with child."

"Nooooo." Alice's tears came again.

James Knight wrapped his arms around his sister and wept himself. "I'm so sorry, Allie, so sorry. I'm so sorry." Was all he could manage.

The doctor lay both forearms across his knees and hung his head. Sometimes being a doctor was awful. He would never forget the night Alice was brought in by her father, beaten and bleeding. Her brother shot twice in the chest on death's door, placed on the bed next to the trembling seventeen-old woman. The memory haunted him worse than anything he'd seen during the war.

The doctor gave her a compassionate smile. "I'm truly sorry."

Alice pulled back from her brother's arms and James pulled out his handkerchief for her. She merely nodded at the doctor. "Thank you, Doctor Reynolds you've been most kind." Her voice trembled.

The doctor nodded and gripped her hand. Alice flinched. The touch of a man, any man except for her father or James, automatically drew fear and made her recoil. She swallowed back that feeling, telling herself, *Doctor Reynolds can be trusted.* She forced herself to look at him and he smiled kindly at her. "Miss Knight, your situation is awful, and if I could change it for you I would, in a heartbeat, but I can't." He looked from her face to her brother's "You're both going to have to find a way to make the best of this. And remember, just because that man was a monster, it doesn't mean the baby is."

Alice's lips trembled.

"For your sake and for the baby's, you have to find a way to forgive and heal and find it in yourself to love the child."

"Reverend and Mrs. Parker said that sometimes God brings unexpected blessings even in horrible situations." Alice tried to encourage herself with her own words. "But I don't know if I can ever love this child." She hung her head. "And what man will ever want me now?"

James squeezed her hand. He'd not been able to shake the anger and guilt since that day. He'd been shot and knocked out, while trying to defend his sister and unable to keep the devastating attack from happening as he lay bleeding on the cabin floor. The guilt burdened his dreams. He blamed himself entirely for not being able to protect her. He swallowed and looked at her, managing a smile for her sake. "You've still got me, and Papa." He knew his words were pointless but he had to say something.

"Not for long. Papa is to be sentenced when the circuit judge arrives and it's likely he'll be hanged." Alice leaned into James and her body shuddered with a sob.

James sighed. "I know. But you'll always have me. I'll keep you safe. I promise." He kissed her forehead. *But I don't blame Papa one bit. Bluster Bill had it coming. If I'd had the chance I'd've killed him too.* He tried hard to fight the hate for Alice's sake. She was going to need him now more than ever. In reality he'd never be able to kill a man, no matter what evil he had done. It just wasn't in him.

Doctor Reynolds nodded. "I am sorry about your father, I know he's a good man. I'm certain he only did what most fathers would do."

Both siblings nodded. "Still, we need to make some plans." James felt defeated. At almost eighteen he was on the precipice of his life, headed to college and ready to take on the world, but his twin sister was much more important, and now he was all she had. *Me and the baby.* He tried to hide his grimace.

"What should we do, Doc?" Alice raised sad eyes to him.

"If it were me, I'd get out of Virginia. Head west, start a new life away from here. Despite this not being your fault in any way, you know what the gossipmongers are like."

"But won't it be just as bad in the west?" James shrugged.

"No one knows you there, so invent a story. Perhaps Alice could be a young war widow with a baby on the way."

"Lie?" Alice frowned.

"Just to begin with, until you get to know people and learn who you can trust. That's the key, learning to trust again. And in time you can tell them the real story."

"No man is ever going to want me if they know the truth." Alice hung her head.

James squeezed her hand. "You don't know that, Allie." He turned to the doctor. "You might be right. I'll take a trip to Harrington and see Papa in the prison. He'll know what we should do."

"I'm coming with you." Alice trembled.

"I don't think that's a good idea. You can stay at the pastorage."

Alice began to tremble. "Please don't leave me. Please."

James sighed and nodded. "Alright, we'll work something out." He smiled at her and took her in his arms. He looked over her head at the doctor. "Thank you, Doc. I appreciate your help and advice, without Papa here we don't have many people on our side."

The doctor nodded. "It's my pleasure, James. Your father is my friend, and it isn't fair how everyone has turned on him and you both. I don't think there's a man in this town that wouldn't have at least considered doing the same, if it were his daughter." He shuddered as he thought of his own fourteen-year-old daughter. "I'm sure the thought would cross my mind." He gave them both a smile. "I'm here to help, whatever you need. The Parkers will be too. There are still a few allies in this town."

"I doubt there will be when the pregnancy becomes obvious." Alice sniffed.

"I wish I could say that wasn't true." The doctor scratched at his chin. "But even in 1865 people are still prone to prejudice and unfounded judgement. That's why I think you should leave. Go somewhere where no one knows you and you can start over."

Both nodded. "You're right, doc."

The doctor turned back to Alice. "I know this isn't a typical pregnancy, but the baby is innocent. Take good care of yourself and be healthy for the child's sake. When he or she is born, you can decide to put the child up for adoption or raise him or her."

"I'm not sure I could raise that monster's baby or ever learn to love it." She managed a courageous smile. "But you're right, regardless of his or her conception." She shuddered but swallowed back the threatening memories. "The child is innocent, and I will do all I can to protect and care for him or her and find a good home where he or she will be loved."

James nodded his agreement. "I'll do whatever I can to help you, Allie. I promise."

The doctor squeezed her hand again and she felt the usual lurch of her body. If the doctor, who she trusted, caused that response how could she ever let a man touch her? *But then who will want me anyway? I'm damaged and spoiled now.* She took a deep breath, lest she become hysterical again. She looked up at the doctor.

"That's probably the best you can do. It's not going to be easy, and it will take time for you to heal and to trust again. But no matter what, give the child every chance at a good life, and try to make the best life you can for yourself."

A very wobbly smile crossed Alice's face. "I will, Doc. I thank you for your kindness."

"My pleasure, if you need anything, let me know, please." The doctor stood. "I really will do all I can to help the two of you. I mean that."

James nodded and helped his sister to her feet. "Thank you. I appreciate it."

The doctor walked them to the door. "Let me know your plans. And if you do resettle, forward us an address so we can keep in touch."

Both siblings nodded and James put his arm around his sister's waist and led her to the wagon.

The doctor leaned against the doorpost and watched them go. "I wish the very best for you both." He shook his head. He felt so helpless. He nodded to Mr. Finch who arrived to have his stitches removed, and followed him inside.

* * * *

"Papa, you look so thin."

Charles Knight gave his daughter a crooked smile. "The food isn't exactly gourmet here." He grimaced, keeping his voice low so the guard watching the visitor space wouldn't hear their conversation.

James eyed his father, new bruises covered the old ones and there was a fresh cut above his eye. He knew the fighting was horrific in the prison. His deep frown caught the older man's eye.

"Son, I know what you're thinking but I'm okay. Truly. It's just the men rough-housing."

"Are you sure, Papa?" Alice lifted a hand to a bruise on his cheek.

"NO TOUCHING!" a stern voice yelled, and the guard thrust a rifle toward Alice. She snatched her hand back and shuddered. Glad they were in a small visitor's room, where they took women. She'd been graciously shielded from being confronted by too many men.

"Sorry, Papa." Tears pooled at the corner of her eyes. "I'm sorry you're in here because of me."

Charles longed to embrace her, but eyeing the guard he gave her a compassionate smile instead. "Alice, you have nothing to feel sorry about. I would make the same choice a hundred times over. I'd rather be hung than have that man alive to hurt someone else. I'm just sorry I couldn't have got to him sooner. I knew he was troubled."

"He was never the same since he came back from the war," James offered.

"Let's not justify his actions, or mention him again." Charles looked at his daughter. "How are you doing, darling?" His throat was tight. There was nothing he could think of that had ever hurt him more than watching her suffer. It was worse than when his wife had died at the hands of a Union soldier who'd burned their home to the ground, decimated their entire crop, and slaughtered the majority of their livestock.

Alice dropped her head and tucked her lips under. She closed her eyes and pulled her shawl tightly around herself. A single sob escaped her lips.

Charles eyes swung to James.

James sighed and put his arm around Alice. "She's pregnant, Papa." He could barely say the words.

Alice buried her head in her brother's chest and sobbed.

A surge of anger pulsed through Charles and he groaned loudly and clenched his fists, trying with all his might to not attract the attention of the guard. He exhaled loudly and closed his eyes. "Oh, darling. I'm sorry."

Alice merely nodded.

"I'll take care of her, Papa. You have my word. I'll protect her and the baby." James drew her close and kissed her hair, rubbing her back as she leaned against his chest. "I'll never fail her again." He closed his eyes and groaned.

"You didn't fail her, Son. You took two bullets to the chest, very nearly gave your life trying to save her. You can't do more than that. She told me in her last letter you've been her rock, the reason she can keep going. She needs you not to blame yourself but to look after her. I'm sorry I'm in here and can't protect her myself."

James nodded. "I thought I might sell the farm and cabin for whatever we can get for it and take her west."

Charles raised his brows.

"Doc Reynolds suggested we find a small town out West somewhere and invent a dead husband, say he died in the war. It's not an uncommon story."

"I don't want to leave, Papa." Alice's voice was barely a whimper.

Charles leaned forward and noticing the guard off to the side smoking a cigarette, he dared to reach forward and squeeze her hand. "You have to go. You can't stay in Virginia just for me. I don't... even know if I'll be here long." He shrugged his shoulders. *She doesn't need to witness my death on top of everything else.* He turned to look at James. "I think that's for the best, Son. Soon the baby will start to show, and you know how people talk. I'm sorry I can't go with you. You know your Mama and I talked of going west before the war." He sighed. *I'm just glad Bonnie wasn't here to witness this, or worse still, for it to happen to her, too.*

James rubbed his sister's back, kissed her hair and looked his father in the eye. "You have my word, sir, that I'll do everything I can to keep her safe."

"I know you will." Charles smiled. "You're a fine man. Make the best life you can for her."

James nodded.

"FIVE MINUTES." The guard spat out.

Charles nodded and closed his eyes. Sighing loudly he paused to think. Knowing this would be the last time he ever saw his precious children, he took a long look at them both. "I'm proud of you, son. You're the man in her life now. Look after her and the baby." He smiled at his daughter and squeezed her hand again. The guard grimaced but ignored it and took another draft on his cigarette.

"Sweetheart, I want you to have the best life you can have. Remember, despite everything, the baby is still a part of you and a part of me. Do everything you can to protect the child and give him or her the best life you can." He smiled at her and lifted his hand to her cheek. The guard merely shrugged. "I wish you happiness and I pray you find a good man someday. One who will love you and the baby. Let the baby know that there are good men in this world and he or she doesn't have to be defined by the circumstances of their origins."

Alice smiled and nodded. "I love you, Papa."

Charles stood and the guard lunged forward with his rifle aimed at him.

Charles appealed to the man. "Please, might I give my daughter one last embrace?"

The guard scowled and the image of his own three daughters entered his mind. He knew Charles' story and wasn't entirely sure he wouldn't have done the same thing in those circumstances. He gave the trio a nod but stood alert.

Alice stood and Charles wrapped her in his arms and held her tightly. He kissed her hair and whispered. "Go with my love and my blessings, darling. Trust your brother, he's young but he's got his head on right. Look after yourself and try to find a way to love and trust again."

She nodded against his chest. "I love you, Papa. I'm sorry for all this. I know I've let you down."

Charles pulled back from her and his eyes lit with fire. He put a hand under her hair and cradled her head. "My darling, there is no truth to that whatsoever. You have not and could never let me down. What has happened is awful, but it does not have to become who you are. You're a Knight and that name means strength and honor, courage and protection. You'll find your strength and your brother will be there for you." He kissed her forehead and stepped back. James put an arm around her and reached a hand out to his father.

Charles gave him a one-armed hug and pulled back with his hand on his son's shoulder. "I'm proud of you, son."

James nodded and blinked away tears. There was no need for any other words. "I'll look after her, Papa. With my life."

"TIMES UP." The guard's voice held just a note of sympathy. Charles nodded and with one more look to his children he turned to the guard. The man clamped the irons back on his wrists.

"Goodbye." He managed a smile and shuffled down the hallway, the chains on his feet clanked on the floor with every step.

Alice lay her head against James' chest and he kissed her hair. "Come on, let's go." He led her to the entrance. "We must take Papa's advice and live the best life we can."

Alice looked up at her brother and gave him a crooked smile. "I will." There was just a hint of hope in her eyes.

Two

Doctor Lane Masters slumped back into his chair and leaned his head back against the canvas wall. He opened his eyes as wide as he could, determined not to fall asleep. When he did the nightmares came. The haunting faces of the men he couldn't save, echoes of soldiers screaming from their makeshift stretchers, legs blown off and faces mangled.

He thrust his arms across his chest. His eyes fell to his father's Bible, peeking out from the pile of papers on his crude desk. He scowled, stood and walked over. Sliding the papers onto the floor he picked up the leather-bound volume. Words he once treasured now seemed meaningless in the eyes of a war he'd never wanted any part of.

He let out a loud sigh and hung his head. Thrusting the book onto his cot, he groaned. The war had been over for nearly a month, but it would still be days before he could go home, they still had wounded men in their crude hospital and he had to wait to be discharged.

"Doctor Masters?" A young man poked his head in the tent.

"What is it, Corporal?"

"Colonel want's you, sir."

Lane took a deep breath. "Did he say why? I'm supposed to be off duty."

"Didn't ask 'im, sir, he just bade me to fetch you."

Lane nodded and lifted his grey coat from the hook. "Tell him, I'll be right there."

"Yes, Captain." The young man nodded and hurried out.

Lane took a deep breath and looked in the faded mirror across the tent. He observed his face as he did up his brass buttons. He looked ten years older than when he'd been conscripted into this rotten war, two years earlier, right out of college. He'd been so enthusiastic and full of hope when he'd graduated from medical school, ready to change the world, and heal all wounds. But only two years in and those dark eyes held no more hope.

The face that stared back at him was weary, and old before his time, he barely recognized himself. What he had seen would never leave him. His training had been all but useless and he'd lost so many more than he could save, and most of those he did save begged for death.

Lane turned from the mirror and reached for his hat. His hand shook as he lifted it to his head. *These hands will never hold a scalpel again.* He scowled at the man in the reflection as if he never wanted to see his image again and walked out to see his Commanding Officer.

He took another deep breath. He did that a lot, swallowing down his thoughts and keeping himself numb, disassociating from the place.

He longed to go home, but his thoughts were conflicted. *Will my home ever be the same? I'm not the same, so how could it be?*

"Are you alright, Doctor?"

Lane jerked his thoughts into line and looked at the young man. "Yes, Private."

The enlisted man nodded and thrust an envelope at Lane. "This came yesterday, it fell out of the mailbag, Sergeant Merton found it when he were takin' the tent down."

Lane frowned and looked at the address. He grimaced. "Ma." A foreboding feeling came over him. His mother seldom wrote, preferring instead to have one of his sisters write on her behalf. But it was unmistakably her writing. The young private stood with his hands behind his back, waiting for his dismissal.

Lane slipped the note out of the envelope and perused it. His face fell and his eyes darkened. He curled up his face and desperately fought the anger and hurt that built up inside him.

"Everything alright, Sir?"

Lane scowled at the young man. "Yes." He lied. "At ease, Private, report to the Colonel. Tell him I'll be right there."

The young man nodded, and turned on his heels to walk away.

Lane lifted the hastily written note and read the words again, barely able to believe it.

Son, I'm sorry to tell ya, Emily has been killed in a train robbery along with her brother Oliver, on their way to

Richmond. Didn't want you to find out from someone else.
I really am sorry, I know you loved her.
  Mama.

  Lane wadded up the note and threw it as far as he could, stifled his growl and shrugged. "So be it," he muttered and a cold numbness swept over him. Automatically he turned and walked toward the Colonel's tent. He stepped inside. "You wanted to see me, Colonel?" His monotone voice held no emotion.

  "Ah, Masters. I need you to oversee the transfer of the last three wounded men to the hospital in Richmond."

  Lane nodded. "Will that be all?"

  "You're being discharged, Doctor. See these men to Richmond then report to the office for your discharge papers."

  Lane merely nodded again.

  The Colonel raised his brows. "I thought that would make you happy, you've made it clear you never wanted to be here."

  Lane shrugged. "What difference does it make?"

  Colonel Yates frowned. "Everything alright, Captain."

  Lane shrugged again. "Yeah."

  The superior officer merely nodded. "The three men are already in the back of the wagon."

  Lane nodded and lifted his hand for another pointless salute for another pointless order.

                    *   *   *   *

"Mama there's a letter from Lane." Fifteen-year-old Dorothy Masters held out the envelopes.

Eliza smiled at her oldest daughter and nodded. "Thank you, dear."

"I hope the boys can come home soon, Mama, the war is over."

Eliza nodded to her daughter. "Me too. Would you make us some tea?" She strode toward the table and sat down.

"Read it out loud." Twelve-year-old Suzannah fetched the cookie jar and sat down at the table. Her mother gave her a mock scowl but nodded her permission.

"Just one Suzy, you'll ruin your supper."

"Yes, Mama."

Eliza took the teacup that Dorothy held out to her and waited for the girl to sit down. She unfolded the brown paper and began to read.

Dear Mama, Papa, Dotty and Suze.

You've no doubt heard by now that I received my official discharge a few weeks ago. I'm sure you're wondering when I can come home.

I met up with Tim at the depot a few days ago. You'll be glad to know he's back on his feet, his leg'll be weak for a while, but I'm just so glad he didn't lose it. Papa needs him on the farm.

I've been doing a lot of thinking and spent some time talking to Tim and to others and, I don't know how to say this but, I won't be coming home.

All three women gasped and tears flooded to Suzannah's eyes. "What? Why not?"

Eliza, sniffed and continued,

I know this will come as a shock to you, but I've decided to head west. I don't expect you to understand but I can't come home, not now. My soul needs time to mend, my spirit is weary and I hope a change of scenery will help. I can't come home knowing Emily isn't there. We were to be married soon and I just can't face it.

I'm leaving medicine behind me. I haven't got the heart to lift a scalpel anymore. You'd know why if you'd lived through what I have. Tim might be able to tell you a few things.

Please don't try to stop me. I'm not the same Lane anymore and home won't be home. I want to remember it as it always was and not the spoiled version of it.

I may return one day, but in the meantime, Misty River, and ya'll remain in my mind and Virginia in my heart.

Your loving, Son and Brother.
Lane.

Eliza put down the letter and reached out to embrace the girls. They wept together quietly and then sat back.

"Will we ever see him again, Mama?"

Eliza gave her youngest daughter a shaky smile. "I don't know, darling, but I do know that war changes people, and he's right to go and find the healing his heart needs."

"I'll miss him." Dorothy dabbed at her eyes.

"We all will, sweetheart, but let's try to be thankful that even if he's not with us, he's alive. If I know Lane, he'll find the healing he needs. He'll turn to the Lord for his comfort. It'll take him time so let's honor his wishes. We will pray for him, every day and hope he'll return to us sometime."

"Reverend Chapman told us that our prayers can cover people even if they are far away, is that true?"

Eliza nodded. "I believe so."

"Then I'll pray so hard he'll be covered all the time."

Eliza nodded. "We all will, darling."

Three

Lane leaned back against the rough leather seat and lifted the newspaper high to block out the sights on the slow-moving train. The corner table in the dining car had become his hiding spot, tucked away behind a cart holding teacups and saucers.

He wasn't reading the paper, at least not actively, it was simply a means of fending off endless small talk while he ate.

"Excuse me." A male voice said. "Excuse me, please."

Lane looked over his paper in the direction of the voice. A young man carefully escorted a young woman into the dining car, edging around others in the cramped car. He led the woman to a table by the back wall about a yard from where he was sitting.

The young man seemed ordinary, perhaps a farmer or a factory worker, but he eyed the young lady who sat facing him. He guessed she was around eighteen or nineteen and she had a soft beauty about her. But it was marred somehow, like she'd been hurt.

He lowered his paper more and watched her, the train lurched, she grimaced and placed her hand on her abdomen.

He lifted the newspaper higher in an attempt to hide his observation of the pair.

"Are you alright, Allie?" James gripped her hand.

Alice nodded and gave him a wobbly smile. "Yes. It's just the train bumps around and makes me feel nauseous."

"And the morning sickness can't be helping."

Lane nodded, his doctor's mind bringing compassionate thoughts. *Poor young woman. I hope she isn't going too far. This travel isn't easy for a mother-to-be.* Catching himself thinking like a doctor again he pulled his thoughts in-line and continued to listen. There was something interesting about that couple. They seemed very young to be married with a baby on the way. But then he supposed that wasn't unusual where he came from.

Alice blushed and looked around. "Should we be talking so openly." She gestured to the few people around them.

James shrugged. "We're never going to see these people again and they're all too busy with their own lives to worry about us. We probably just look like a young couple to them."

Alice wrinkled her nose. "Are you going to tell people we're a married couple?" She swallowed back another wave of nausea as a waitress walked past with a coffeepot.

"Of course not, we'll tell the truth, you're my sister."

"How will we explain the baby?" She lowered her voice.

"We can solve that problem when we settle somewhere. We'll invent a husband for you."

Alice hung her head and her lip trembled. "I don't like to lie."

"Would you rather tell people what really happened? About the attack?"

Lane shuddered and closed his eyes. *That poor girl.* He fought the swirling memories. This wasn't the first unfortunate woman he'd encountered. It seemed there were far too many in her situation. War brought with it all kinds of unspeakable evil. He finished his coffee and realized he hadn't turned a page for a time. So, he flicked the paper and turned his head to look at the opposite page, but he didn't read a word. He knew he shouldn't be listening, but what harm could it do? He was never going to see them again. Besides, it took his mind off his own broken heart.

Alice shook her head and dabbed at a tear in the corner of her eye. "Of course not. Papa said we had to make the best life we could. I can't do that with everyone knowing I'm spoiled."

James gripped her hand again. "Stop, saying that, Allie." He paused and looked up at the waitress who delivered his tea and her cup of milk. She placed toast with just a skim of butter before Alice, it was all she could stomach on the lurching train.

James offered her some of his roast meal, but she grimaced and shook her head, lifting the toast to her mouth instead.

James swallowed his mouthful and turned back to her. "You aren't spoiled. An evil man attacked you, that's all, there's no shame in that."

Alice smiled at him and sipped her milk. "You're a good, kind brother, James, but you know as well as I do that no man will want me if they know the truth."

"That's not true."

Alice raised her brows. "Would you want someone like me?"

James sucked in a breath and bit his lips together, his pause said everything.

"Just as I thought."

He furrowed his brow and touched her hand. "Allie, I could absolutely love someone like you. It would take extra special care to be worthy of a heart so trampled. But it would be wonderful to see her blossom and trust again. That's what I pray for you."

Alice nodded, he was kind to humor her. Something occurred to her. "I'm going to need a new name."

"What do you mean?"

"If I'm a widow, you and I can't have the same last name, and before we arrive, I'll have to change into mourning clothes. We'll never get away with it otherwise." She sighed. "I do so hate to deceive people."

Lane grimaced. *No, but I can't blame you one bit, I would do the same for my sister.*

"Allie, it won't be forever. I'm sure in time when we get to know people and you feel safe and trust again you can share the real story."

Allie nodded. "So, what should I be called? We can't both be Knight."

"How about you be Knight and I'll change my name."

"No that's not necessary. What about I take Mama's name?"

"Mrs. Alice Cole, and your husband died at Manasses, you'd been married less than a year."

She grimaced. "I'm not even eighteen yet. Is that really a believable story?"

"Mama was sixteen when she and Papa married."

"True, and had you and I when she was seventeen." She curled her mouth up. "I guess that's something we'll have in common." She sighed.

"You'll be eighteen before the baby arrives." He finished his meal and looked up at her. "You know twins run in the family. There was us and Ma's sisters and she told me their great grandmother was a twin too."

Alice's eyes grew wide and her mouth dropped. "It's hard enough to think about one baby."

"Sorry, I shouldn't have said that." He watched her push away her plate and sit back and close her eyes. "Are you alright?"

"Yes, but I'm done. I think I'd like to lie down."

James frowned. "I'm sorry the best I can do is sitting up in the train. We should've gotten a private car."

"Nonsense, we need the money from the farm to set us up somewhere else. I'll be fine, I promise."

He nodded and stood, pulled some coins from his pocket and lay them on the table. He helped his sister stand and made sure she was steady.

Just as she stepped away from the table the waitress came through the narrow passageway from the next car and crashed right into her.

"Ooooohfff." Alice collapsed to her hands and knees.

"Oh, Miss. I'm so sorry." The woman knelt down on the other side as James looked at her with concern.

"That's okay. I'm fine." Alice smiled at the waitress. The woman nodded and gave her a contrite smile, hurrying away to serve the next customer.

James squatted down. "Are you alright?"

"I just want to sit for a moment. My head is spinning."

James nodded. "Can I get you anything?"

It was impulse or instinct or merely habit that made Lane put down his paper and stand up. He snatched a cup of water from the nearby cart and squatted down in front of her.

Alice sat back and leaned away from him. Her eyes wide and her lips trembling.

James frowned at Lane and he moved back just slightly in the cramped space. "I'm sorry, I just wanted to offer the lady a glass of water." He held it up but she wouldn't dare reach for it.

James took the glass and nodded his thanks.

"Thank you."

"You're welcome. She should just sit for a moment, then take her back to her seat and try to get some rest."

James squinted at him. He wanted to ask many questions but instead he merely nodded and thanked the stranger.

Lane nodded, gave Alice a compassionate smile and stood. "I hope you feel better soon, Ma'am." Without waiting for a response, he turned and hurried back to his small cabin at the back of the train. Slumping back against the uncomfortably hard chair, he groaned and chastened himself. "No matter how tragic a case, you can't go back to medicine." He shuddered as the images of the crude operating conditions of war circled his brain.

He grimaced and yawned. He knew he couldn't fight sleep forever, but he wasn't looking forward to another sleepless night haunted by his memories.

*   *   *   *

James guided Alice carefully into the small hotel room, the busboy followed with their two suitcases. As soon as he unlocked the door, James led Alice to the bed and helped her lie down. He slipped off her shoes and lay a blanket over her. She fell asleep almost immediately.

James turned to the busboy who was still waiting for his tip. "I'm sorry..." He peered at the boy's name tag. "Oliver, my sister is exhausted, it's very late and we've been traveling for three days. She's barely slept."

Oliver nodded.

James put his hand in his pocket and pulled out a quarter. He passed it to the boy and a wide smile crossed his face. "Thank ya, Mista"

"You're welcome." He walked the boy to the door and closed it behind him, locking it firmly. He turned to observe the room, it only had one large bed, but it didn't worry him, he knew Alice would prefer him to be close anyway. He slipped off his shoes and climbed up on the other side of the bed, pulling a separate blanket over himself. He turned on his side toward his sister and put his hand on her arm, so that she'd know he was there.

He looked at her face in the low lamplight. She was very pale and he knew she desperately needed sleep. He was glad he'd insisted they get off the train and rest for a while. He squeezed her arm and stretched his neck to kiss her forehead. "Goodnight, Allie. You are quite safe." He wouldn't dare turn out the lamp, even when he was right beside her. Since the attack she hadn't liked to be alone or in the dark, especially in a place she didn't know.

He lay awake and thought about what was coming for her. He whispered a prayer, hoping the words would soothe and bless her. "Lord, protect my sister, help me to keep her safe. I pray she can have a good life, despite what happened. Help me to know how to care for her. I ask that you help her to heal and learn to trust again and overcome the fear. I want to see her loved by a good man, who'll love the child too, no matter its circumstances.

"Please keep her well." He grimaced and ended with, "she and the baby are all the family I have now." He squeezed her arm again and closed his eyes.

Four

"Shimmer Lake, next stop, Shimmer Lake." The conductor walked through the train calling out in every car.

Lane reached under his seat and collected his small bag. He stayed seated until the train lurched to a halt amidst gushes of steam and screeches of brakes.

He waited for a group of ladies to pass by before he stood and followed them out. Leaping out of the train he stepped up and put his hand out to an older woman who gave him a smile, lifted her skirts and stepped out. He made sure she was steady on her feet and gave her a nod.

He wandered over to wait for the baggage to be unloaded. Walking into the station he gestured to the clerk and strode up to the desk. "How far to Shimmer Lake Township?"

"Bout fifty miles as the crow flies, ain't got a spur there yet." The young man stated and scooped up a grizzly toddler pulling at his trouser legs. "Stage leaves at noon." He pointed to the other side of the station where the stagecoaches waited.

Lane glanced up at the clock and nodded. He had a half hour wait, and he'd never yet heard of a stage being on time. He smirked and went in search of his two suitcases.

Finding a quiet spot to wait he sat down and pulled out the slip of paper he'd torn from a newspaper. He opened it again and gripped its jagged edges. He perused it.

Clerk Wanted for weekly newspaper. Duties include setting type, taking orders, and delivering newspapers. Must be able to read and write and follow instructions.

He looked up abruptly as the stage came around the corner. He pulled out his pocket watch and chuckled. Five minutes early. "Well, there's a first time for everything." He shoved the newspaper deep in his pocket and stood to wait for the arriving stage.

*　　*　　*　　*

Alice sat up on the bed leaning against the wall. She closed her eyes as her head swirled and her stomach churned. James passed her a cup of chamomile tea the porter had just brought to their room.

"Thank you." She managed a shaky smile.

"Allie. You obviously aren't well, we need to get you to the doctor."

"I'll be alright. The tea is settling my stomach. We don't need to spend the money. I'm sure this will pass."

"Allie!" James raised his brows at her. "I'm not going to argue. I'm taking you to a doctor, today. I don't care if I have to sell my shoes to do so."

Alice nodded. "I have been experiencing some bleeding."

James eyes grew wide. "Allie. Why didn't you tell me?"

"I don't want to be a burden, you've already had to turn your life upside down for me...." She hung her head.

James took the empty cup from her and lay it down on the table. He climbed up on the bed and took her hand. "Look at me." His voice was calm.

She lifted contrite eyes to him.

"Alice Elizabeth Knight, you listen to me now. I love you. You're my sister, my best friend and the only family I have in the whole world. I would give my life for you. You're not a burden to me. I just want to know you and the baby are safe and well. Life hasn't gone the way we expected but you're more important to me than going to college. I promised Mama and Papa that I would always make sure you're safe and I mean to do just that." He kissed her forehead. "I don't know what I'd do without you."

Alice smiled at him and leaned against his chest. He put his arms around her and kissed her hair again.

"I love you too, James, you're the best brother a girl could ask for."

James nodded. "Now, let me help you and I'll hire a carriage to take you to a doctor. No arguments, I don't care how much it costs."

Alice nodded, shuffling to the edge of the bed so James could help her with her boots. He fetched her black shawl to go with the widow's garb. They might as well get in character now. He took her arm and led her to the lobby. Seating her as close to the counter as he could, he squatted before her. "I'm going to the counter to see if I can book a carriage. I'll be right there, alright. You're quite safe."

Alice took a deep breath. She had to get used to this sooner or later. He was so considerate of her feelings and she felt so safe with her brother. She nodded and he squeezed her arm and walked to the counter. Alice sat back and closed her eyes, she tipped her head back against the wall.

A gentleman walking past observed her pale face and bent down to touch her shoulder. "Ma'am are you..."

Alice sat bolt up and thrust her arms over her head. "No, get away from me!"

The bewildered man stepped back and Alice began to sob.

James pivoted on his heels immediately and tore across the room to the spot. The gentlemen standing before her had a helpless look on his face. James knelt and put his arms around her. "Shhh. You're safe. I've got you."

"I really am sorry, sir. Is that your wife? I just saw her sitting there and she looked unwell. I wanted to see if she was alright. I meant no harm."

James pivoted so he could look at the man. Still holding his trembling sister close. "It's alright, I know you were just trying to help. She's my sister and she's been through something very traumatic. It's going to take her time to trust people again, especially strangers. I don't like to leave her alone if I can help

31

it, she just needed to rest for a moment while I order a carriage."

"Oh. I am sorry. I didn't mean to cause upset. Is there anything I can do to help?" The man's eyes held genuine compassion.

Alice calmed and James sat back from her, standing to greet the man. "There is one thing if you don't mind. I was trying to book a carriage to get my sister to the doctor, oh and you might suggest a good doctor."

The man smiled. "It just so happens that my uncle is a doctor in this town. I have a carriage out front and I can take you there if you like."

"We couldn't ask you to do that, sir, you don't even know us."

The man nodded. "Henry Augustus Bartholomew Clementine." He got the usual response, a look of amusement from James. "Yes, that's my real name but my friends just call me Clem. And you didn't ask, I offered."

James put his hand out to the young man. "James Knight. I'm sorry my name isn't nearly as fancy as yours. And this my sister... uh... Mrs. Alice... uh Cole." He stammered a bit.

Clem frowned slightly but said nothing. He looked down at Alice who had calmed but still eyed him tentatively. He squatted down so he was eye level with her and put a tentative hand out to shake. "A pleasure to meet you, Mrs. Cole. I'm Clem, ma'am and I'm very sorry I frightened you."

James observed Alice to see what she would do. He could see her lips trembling, but she squared her shoulders and put a shaky hand out to his. Knowing James was there gave her courage.

"It's... ahhh... it's nice to meet you, Sir. And I'm very sorry I reacted like that." She quickly snatched back her hand.

The man lifted his hand and smiled. "There is no need for you to apologize, I understand completely. When you're ready I've offered my carriage to take you and your brother to the doctor."

"Thank you, that's most kind." Alice managed a smile, determined to take her father's advice and make the best of her life, that meant she had to get past the fear and learn to trust again. It was scary, working through the trauma but with James nearby she knew she could manage.

Clem stood up. "Can I get you both something to eat or drink?"

"That won't be necessary," James protested.

"Please, it would be my pleasure. Coffee and a muffin perhaps?"

James turned to Alice. She shook her head and rubbed her stomach. "Just chamomile tea please and a piece of toast with a skim of butter, if it's not, too much of a bother. It seems to be all I can manage at the moment."

Clem squinted at her and gave James a knowing look.

"She's in the family way."

Clem smiled. "I understand." It was on the tip of his tongue to say congratulations but there was something about them both and their manner that was familiar to him and made him hesitate. "Very well, chamomile it is. For you James?"

"Coffee, and a muffin sounds wonderful." He reached into his pocket.

Clem put a hand out to stop him. "Please, it's on the house." He grinned and pivoted on his heels.

James sat down and watched the man. But he didn't go to the counter to make the order, he strode past and through the double swinging door that said, 'Staff only.' He frowned and then his eyes swung to the large sign above the counter. 'Clementine's Hotel and Restaurant. He chuckled internally, *I guess I was too worried about Allie to make the connection.*

James turned to her and gave her a smile. "Are you alright now."

"Yes, I'm sorry you have to come to my rescue..."

James put a hand up to stop her. "Allie, you never have to apologize. I know what you've been through, I don't mind being here for you. I was proud of you though for shaking his hand, especially after he frightened you."

Alice smiled at him. "I have to get better sometime, and Mama always said the only way to get past something difficult is to go through it. If I keep hiding I'm never going to get any better. So, with you by my side I'm going to try to take more steps through the pain."

James leaned over and kissed her forehead. "You're a tough cookie, Alice Knight..." he eyed Clem who placed a tray before them, hoping he hadn't caught his slip of the tongue. *I have to be more careful.*

Clem walked out through the double doors and leaned against the wall for just a moment. He took a deep breath and exhaled loudly. He'd seen a woman like that before, his fiancée. Some years back she'd been attacked by a man and had conceived a child by him. Only when she found out about the child she took her own life. He took another deep breath and exhaled it slowly, attempting to push back down the carefully buried feelings. Lydia had been gone three years and he still was not over it. *I loved her and I would've loved her and the child, regardless. I wish I could've told her that, perhaps she'd still be alive. Alice is a brave and resilient girl.* He couldn't be certain that was what Alice had been through, but she responded the same way Lydia had. Flinching at anyone's touch, shifty eyes, never really trusting anyone.

He lifted his eyes to petition God on Alice's behalf. He'd found the Lord soon after Lydia had died when he'd stumbled into a church desperate for comfort. There he'd found not just comfort, but the Great Comforter. "Thank you, Lord, and be with Alice." He nodded. Leaving the situation in God's hands was all he could do. He was determined to do all he could to help them. In a way it was if he was helping Lydia.

Exhaling again he continued into the kitchen. "Cass, Might I have some chamomile tea and some dry toast

35

with just a skim of butter, a cup of coffee with milk and sugar and whatever is your best muffin today."

Cass looked at him and smiled. "Certainly, will that be all?"

"Yes, thank you. And that's on me."

"I understand, sir." She nodded.

"Cass?" Clem tipped his head to her.

"I'm sorry, I understand, Clem."

"Thank you, you can call my father, sir. I'm just Clem."

She nodded and hurried to tray up the order. "Which room is it for?" She laid the tray down and rang the bell.

"No need for that, I'll take it. I've made some new friends, they're just in the lobby."

"You know you don't have to serve, sir... Ah, Clem. You have staff for that."

"Cass, I can't expect my employees to do a job I wouldn't be prepared to do myself."

Cass nodded, this was her first week on the job and it was already the best job she ever had. No more eeking out a pathetic living in little more than a shack. Her two children could eat properly now and she was on her way to affording a decent place for them to live. Maybe this year she'd afford to get them new clothing so they might go to school. *That's all I want for them. Thanks to Mr. Clementine it might actually happen.*

She passed the tray to Clem and he headed back to the lobby. Catching James's slip of the tongue as he placed the tray down, he nodded. That confirmed his suspicions, and he determined to look after them both for as long as they stayed at his hotel. *For Lydia.* "Do you mind if I join you for a time?"

"We don't want to take up your time, sir." James passed Alice the teacup.

Clem frowned. "You don't need to call me, sir, and it's my pleasure to spend time with the people in my hotel. I really do see it as my ministry."

"It's lovely." Alice sipped at her tea and then bit into the toast.

He smiled. "Thank you. I've got a good team."

"Do you live here?"

"Some of the time." Clem shrugged. "Actually, I'm handing it over to my cousin soon. I'm setting up another hotel, branching out, so to speak. It'll be my fifth. I plant them, spend some time building them and getting them established and then build another."

"Five? Here in Craigstown?" James eyes grew wide.

"No. I started with a small hotel in Chicago, with my father, actually. He has a chain of hotels and he sent me out to 'the prairies' to start more. This is the biggest one. I have four others in small towns and I'm in the process of building one in the smallest town yet. It should be finished by September. I'm hoping it'll help the town to grow and thrive. It's in an idyllic tranquil spot next to a large lake, with mountains in the background. I like the town so much I'm considering settling down there for a time. I think I could enjoy a quiet country life. My mother would be pleased I'm finally considering settling down although, I'm sure she'd wish I chose Chicago or somewhere closer to her."

Both siblings nodded.

"So where are you both headed?"

James scrambled for an answer. "Well, uhh. We aren't too sure yet. We had a farm back in Virginia, and Alice...uhhh... lost her husband in the war so, we thought it best to head West and find a new life for ourselves. Start over, so to speak, but we don't know where yet. I was thinking perhaps Montana. But we won't move on until I'm sure Allie is alright. We stopped here and got off the train because she wasn't well."

Clem's eyebrows flew up. "Montana you say?"

James shrugged and swallowed a too-big bite of muffin. "I've heard it's nice out there and the homesteading is good. We have the money from selling our farm so we can pick up a piece of land easily. I hope to go to a surveyor in a few days and look at what's available on the plains."

An excited gleam shone in Clem's eyes and he grinned. "Might I make a suggestion?"

"Sure." James smiled and Alice merely nodded finishing her tea and toast, opting to let the men discuss it.

"The little town I just set up my hotel in is in Montana, it's called Shimmer Lake, and it might be ideal for you both. It has homesteading land all around."

"We just want to go somewhere small. It's a quiet life for us."

"Shimmer Lake has less than two hundred people. Good decent folk, lots of families moving that way."

James turned to Alice. "What do you think?"

Alice shrugged. "I don't know. I trust you to decide."

James nodded. "It sounds ideal." Then he glanced at his sister and grimaced. "Does the town have a doctor?"

Clem frowned. "Not yet, I don't believe. But there is a woman who's a retired nurse. I only know that because she stitched a cut on my wrist.' He pulled up his sleeve so they could see the large purple scar that ran up his forearm.

"What happened?"

Clem chuckled. "I got a little too hands-on with the building. Got bit by a saw."

James smiled. "Where is the closest doctor?"

"I'm not sure, but perhaps we can work on getting a doctor for the town before the need arises." He gestured to Alice.

"We'll have time to work it out. She's due early November. We hope to be well and truly settled before the winter sets in." James glanced out at the June sunshine. James turned to Clem. "You might just be the answer to prayer we need, Mr. Clementine." He looked at Alice. "Are you ready to go?"

"Yes, I feel a little better now."

James helped her to her feet and Clem escorted them out the door and into his carriage.

Five

James and Alice strolled out into the foyer of the doctor's rooms. Clem sat patiently reading the newspaper. He looked up as the siblings approached. "You didn't have to wait, Clem. We could've hired a carriage back to the hotel."

"Nonsense. It's the least I can do. And I've taken care of the medical bills. You need not worry."

"There was no need, we can pay our way." James seemed a little hurt.

Clem looked him in the eye. "Please, I'd like to." It was confession time. "I uhhh.... knew someone in your sister's... situation and... well... she isn't here anymore. I'd like to do what I can to help you, since I can't help her."

Alice looked horrified, how had he guessed?

Clem dared put a hand gently on her arm and she flinched but willed herself not to react. Her heart rate rose a little. "Ma'am, your secret is safe with me, and I don't believe anyone else needs to know. I only know because I saw the same signs in a friend who was attacked by a man. I'm truly sorry for how you've suffered."

Alice bit her lip and looked at him. "Thank you, that's kind." A tear escaped and she swiped at it. "It's taking me time to learn to trust."

"Of course it is. You're a strong and brave woman, Miss Knight... ahhh, Mrs. Cole." He gave her an understanding smile. "I'm afraid my fiancée wasn't as brave."

"You're fiancée?" James's voice was full of compassion. They began walking out to the carriage.

James helped Alice up and climbed up after her. Clem climbed in and took the seat opposite. He swallowed and looked at them. "She took her own life when she found out about the baby. She said in the letter she left for me that she could never raise a monster's baby and didn't want me to have the obligation of taking her on." He shuddered, he'd never said those words out loud before and he could barely get them out now. "She wasn't as strong as you, and she didn't know the Lord, neither did I back then."

"That's why I can manage." Alice grimaced. "Most of the time, and because of James. I couldn't do this without him."

"Sure, you could." James said. "You're a strong woman."

"I wasn't strong enough to fight him off though." Alice's body shook.

"Don't do that Allie. Don't blame yourself."

Alice looked up at her brother and nodded. She turned to look at Clem, daring to ask, "Did you put her off when you found out?"

Clem frowned. "What do you mean?"

"I mean, after the man... the attack... the incident. Did you put her off, break the engagement?"

He shook his head. "Of course not."

"Would you've married her anyway?"

41

"Anyway? You imply there was something wrong with her."

Alice hung her head. "Didn't you feel like she was spoiled? Weren't you repulsed by her and that man's baby?"

Clem smiled. "Alice." She looked up at him. "I loved her all the more, because she had suffered so. And I would've loved that baby. I didn't know about the baby until after she'd taken her life. Her mother took her to the doctor, and she didn't want me to know. I've thought about her a lot since then and no, I wasn't repulsed and she certainly wasn't spoiled.

"I never thought of the baby as that man's. I wanted him to have no power over either of our lives. I thought of the baby as a part of Lydia and so in need of love. I guess I'd just come to the Lord, too and He helped me overcome my anger and hurt." He touched her hand again and this time she didn't feel the lurch, she was feeling more comfortable with him. "If you're asking if you think a man could love you after what happened and love the baby, then I say yes, if they are the right man. It wouldn't have made a difference to me. I just wanted to love her through it."

Alice smiled and nodded. She wiped away a tear. "Thank you. I'm sorry for asking such personal questions. It's just I've never known of anyone else in my... situation... and I have to admit I'm frightened about what the future holds." She lay her hand on stomach. At four months along she was beginning to show, at least when she pressed her skirts tight against her. "For both of us."

"That's what I'm here for." James said.

"And I'd like to be, too." Clem offered.

Alice gave him an uncertain look.

"I just mean as a friend. I'm engaged again and my fiancée will be moving out to Shimmer Lake with me. We'll live there for a time, get the hotel established then most likely move further west and start another."

Alice smiled.

"For some reason the Lord halted me when I saw you in the foyer. He drew me to you, and I felt compelled to meet you both. Now I know why. He wanted to use my experience to support you. I'm most grateful that I can use my past to benefit another. Isn't it like God to bring good things from bad situations."

Alice smiled. "Mama used to say that a lot. Thank you, Mr. Clementine. You're most kind. Yes, I believe the Lord did send you our way today and I'm grateful."

"Clem, please."

Alice nodded. "Clem."

James looked at Clem. "When are you planning to go West?"

"A month or so." Clem nodded. "I plan to supervise the completion of the hotel."

"The doctor said Alice is to take it easy for a few weeks, stay in Craigstown and for her to get her rest...." James grimaced. "Our savings are really going to take a hit."

"I'd be honored if you'd stay in my suite as my guests. I have four rooms and no one to share them with. Then when you're well enough, I'd be delighted to accompany you out to Shimmer Lake. Quite frankly I'd love the company."

"We couldn't ask that of you." Alice felt quite overwhelmed. "I don't... know..."

He smiled at her. "I can assure you, you will be quite safe and you didn't ask it of me. I'm just offering myself as a servant of Christ. Let me do this for you both, in honor of Lydia?"

Alice looked at her brother. James shrugged. "It's up to you. I'd sleep on a barn floor if it was just me."

Alice turned to look at their new benefactor and friend. She gave him a genuine smile. "Thank you, that is most kind."

Clem smiled. "It'll be wonderful having you both. I don't have many friends as you can imagine, moving around so much as I do. Just Missy. She's a tough girl too. Lost her Papa in the war and came west all on her own to teach. I met her at the mission church I attend."

"She's a teacher?"

Clem smiled at Alice as the carriage pulled to a stop. "Yes. A fine one. She teaches the fifth grade at Craigstown Public School. I hope she might get a job at Shimmer Lake."

"I'm sure she will, God always has things worked out." She placed her hand on her stomach, glad to not have to lie, at least to one person. She took James' hand and he helped her down from the carriage. "He

44

can even bring joy from a tragedy. When I went to the doctor I thought I was losing the baby. At first, I thought it would be a good thing. It might make my life easier and help me to forget. But then when the doctor told me there was a very real possibility that if I don't rest for a time and get my strength back that I could lose the baby, I suddenly felt protective of him or her. Does that sound strange?"

"Not at all, it sounds just like a mother loving HER child." Clem put an emphasis on her. He touched her arm. "Because that's who this is. YOUR child and no one else's, except for the man that you marry someday then it will be his child, too. The circumstances of the baby's conception don't matter when love is involved."

Alice felt an overwhelming surge of hope rush through her and impulsively she put her arms out and embraced him.

James' eyes widened and Clem smiled as he patted her back.

Alice stood back abruptly. "I'm sorry."

"Don't be, no one should ever apologize for a hug. It was brave of you."

She trembled. "I'm surprised myself. Suddenly you made me feel hopeful. You're the only one besides James and Papa that have been kind to me and made me feel like I could actually have a bright future after all, and that man doesn't get to take my life from me."

"I'm glad. The Lord really did bring us all together for a purpose."

Alice smiled and tried to slow her heart-rate. That was enough stepping through the fear for one day.

"Come on, I'll show you where you can stay." He led them into the lobby of the hotel and up to the desk. "Jack," he called to the concierge. The man stood, ran his hand down his waistcoat and walked over, his eyes wide with anticipation.

"Jack this is Mr. James Knight and his sister, Mrs. Cole. They are friends of mine and are to be given VIP treatment. They'll be joining me in my suite. Please see to it that two extra meals be provided along with a good supply of fresh milk and chamomile tea."

Jack turned his eyes to the two young people. *She's very young to be a widow.* But he eyed her black clothing and nodded. "As you wish, sir."

"Clem, please."

Jack nodded.

"And there is to be no bill." He raised his brows.

James and Alice blushed.

Jack nodded again. "As you wish." He hurried away to action the orders.

"I need to fetch my things from our room upstairs." Alice stated.

"No problem." Clem reached across and hit a bell twice. Two bellboys showed up. "Ah, Terry and Benjamin." He frowned. "Tuck your shirt in, lad, we don't want to look scruffy around here." His voice wasn't unkind.

Benjamin blushed. "Yes, sir, sorry, sir."

Clem smiled. "No harm done, just check your uniform before you come to the lobby. I need the two of you to fetch the bags from room..." He looked at James.

"Twelve."

Clem turned back to the busboys. "Fetch the cases from room twelve and have them brought to my suite."

"Your suite, sir?"

"Yes, Terry, to my suite."

Terry nodded and the two boys hurried away.

Clem chuckled. "You'd think I was the king by the way they get so nervous around me. I know I'm the boss, but I hope I'm not that frightening."

Six

Lane jumped down the final step of the stagecoach and onto the rough-hewn wooden platform. He reached back for his bags and nodded to the driver. He'd had the stage to himself since the train depot.

Pausing for a moment to look around, it was a perfectly normal, nondescript town just like so many others on the frontier. It seemed awfully sleepy and that suited him just fine. He wasn't here for adventure or action. He'd had enough of that for a lifetime.

Looking up the street a ways, he saw a sign that said, Clementine's Hotel and Restaurant. He frowned, below the sign was written, 'opening soon.' "Hmmm." He muttered aloud. He looked across the road. There was a saloon at the far end of town and a small boarding house next door to the mercantile.

"The boarding house it is then." He shrugged.

*   *   *   *

Mrs. Harvey put down the scrubbing brush when the door opened and sat back on her feet. She swiped her forearm across her hot forehead and stood, stretching her back. She looked up at the stranger and smiled. "Good day."

Lane returned her polite smile. "Good day, ma'am. I don't mean to be interruptin' ya work, but I was told this here was a boarding house and ya might have

48

room for me." He affected an accent, hoping he might blend in.

The woman didn't seem convinced, as though she could tell his accent was put on. She said nothing, merely nodded and gestured for him to follow her, buttoning up her sleeve as she walked into a large dining room. She gestured for him to sit then lifted a large ledger from the small sideboard.

She flicked open to a clean page. "Ya on ya own?"

"Ahh... Yeah. It's just me."

She nodded and eyed his clothing. "A dollar a week, cludin' meals." Her voice was hopeful, as though she expected push back.

"That sounds right reasonable, ma'am."

The woman's eyes widened and she smiled. It was twice what she normally charged but business was down and she had to make a living somehow, especially with the new hotel about to open. She continued. "Pay a week in advance and if ya ain't gonna be here for meals, let me or Polly know."

"Polly?"

"She's the cook and maid. This is too much 'ouse for just me."

Lane nodded. "That sounds good." He reached into his pocket and pulled out five dollars. "This should cover me till I can find somethin' more permanent like."

Mrs. Harvey squinted at him. "What's ya name."

"Masters."

"Where're ya from Mr. Masters?"

"East." It was all he was ready to admit to.

"Were ya in the war?"

Lane closed his eyes and shuddered. "Yes'm, but I'd just as soon not talk about it."

"Alright, I meant no harm. Ya'll be in room five. Follow me."

She led him through a door and they passed through a large living room and up a wide staircase. The stout woman tried to hide her exertion as she climbed but Lane noticed the strain to her breathing.

They stepped out onto a landing then entered a wide hallway. Black numbers were painted onto each sunflower yellow door. "This'n 'ere." She pushed open the door marked, 'five' and led him inside. "Only one wif' a balcony, overlooks the 'ole street."

"It's very nice." He took a moment to look around. The large room had a rather lumpy looking bed and wide French doors that led onto a large balcony. Two chairs and a small table sat outside the door. The room had a rather over-sized desk with a stuffed chair, two armoires and a tall wardrobe with a mirror on the front. He nodded. "Thank ya, ma'am, this'll do just fine."

"Last chap what stayed 'ere was a writer, were here for three months while he wrote 'im a 'ole book. 'bout the frontier 'e said." She opened the cupboard as she spoke. "I says to 'im, do you think folks back in the east wanna know what goes on in our little town? But 'e said they do. Said we was a 'cur... i...os.. ity.' She struggled to get her tongue around the word.

Lane nodded. "I suppose I can understand that." He clenched his teeth and grimaced as he realized he'd forgotten the accent. Oh, well, he couldn't keep that up forever.

Mrs. Harvey squinted at him and tilted her head to the side. "Ya city raised?"

"No ma'am but I did attend college in the city, for a time."

"What'd ya learn?"

"Med... uhh... literature."

The woman squinted again. There was more to this man that he was letting on. "Why'd ya 'ide ya proper voice? I know'd ya ain't from these parts soon as I looked at ya. Ain't no one round 'ere got cloth like that." She gestured to his clothing he'd purchased with his final pay from the army.

"I'm sorry, I guess I was hoping to fit in and stay anonymous."

"Anon...e mouse?" The woman raised her brows.

"Stay unknown."

"What ya runnin' from?"

"Nothing really, I just want a chance to start over."

"Alright, it's ya own buznuss." She opened the doors to air the room out. "Ya be need'n anything else?"

"No thank you, ma'am.

"Very well, Mr. Masters. I'll leave ya to it. Bathroom's yonder three rooms down from 'ere on the left. Got indoor plumin'." Her face evidenced her pride in that fact. She'd recently had it installed in a hope she'd be able to compete with the new hotel. "Supper's at seven."

"Thank you." He tipped his head to her. The woman pivoted on her heels and left the room.

Lane closed the door and shook his head. "Fakery never seems to fool anyone. I guess I can't deny my city years. At least they don't have to know I was a doctor. That part of life is behind me, once and for all." He lifted his small suitcase onto one of the armoires. He'd deal with unpacking later. He flopped onto the bed, hanging his feet over the edge so he didn't have his shoes on the covers. He could already hear the scolding from his mother in his ears.

He lay back and closed his eyes. "I'm here. Now what?" He shrugged. "Tomorrow I'll look for the gazette office, see if I can't get myself that job."

Lane stood and walked to the doors, pushed one open and stepped out onto the balcony. He slumped down in the rocker and looked over the town. He shrugged again. "It's as good a place as any to start over." He closed his eyes and rocked gently as the June sun shone on his face.

*   *   *   *

"It's so peaceful here." Alice lifted the teacup to her lips and leaned back against the trunk of the oak trying to get her stomach to settle.

Missy Branson pricked the potatoes cooking in the cast iron pot over the fire and resumed her seat on the blanket opposite her, layin. "Yes, it is. I can't wait till we get to Shimmer Lake. Clem tells me it's beautiful."

Alice smiled and they looked across at the two men fishing, subconsciously rubbing her rounding

stomach. The nausea had been bad that day. "He's a generous man, paying our way, and setting up a wagon for us." She smiled. The two women were to share the bigger of the two wagons for their first night on the trail. Alice had never seen such luxurious and elaborate wagons in her life. Clem had spared no expense. They couldn't take all their belongings by stage and this way they could take their time and travel at their own pace, especially with Alice's condition. Still James and Clem had thought it better they leave while Alice was in her fifth month, too much later and it would become much harder.

"Yes." Missy smiled. "Clem's been through a lot, but he lets God lead him and he's a wonderful man. I can't wait for us to be married."

Alice smiled at the woman. "Have you set a date?"

"Not yet, we want to settle in the town for a time. I guess I'll take a room at a boarding house somewhere while he gets established. He wants to build us a house so we don't have to live at the hotel."

"Well, I'm glad I'll at least know two people in the town, and James of course."

Missy smiled. "Me, too. Do you plan to farm."

"Homestead, I suppose. But we might have to live in a boarding house for a time too. Least till we find something. James wants me to be close to town so I can get help for when the baby comes." She bit her lip and closed her eyes. She hadn't meant to talk about the baby to a woman she'd only known a few days.

Missy's eyes widened and she smiled. She knew Alice was expecting but it seemed there was

something unusual about the pregnancy since they didn't talk about it much. So she said nothing until Alice brought it up. She smiled. "It's good that we'll take the journey very slow. When are ya due?" She was relieved she could finally talk about it.

Alice tried to smile as she nodded. "Mmmhmm. 'bout November I reckon."

Missy put her hand out to grip Alice's. "I'm happy for ya. Sorry for ya loosing ya husband though, Clem told me he died in the war, at Manasses."

Alice flinched. *Happy for me? You wouldn't be if you knew. Obviously Clem hasn't told her that.* "I ahhhh..." She managed a shaky smile. "Thank you. And yes, Cooper was a good husband. I miss him." She said quickly as though getting the lie out fast made it less untrue. But the fewer people that knew of her shame the better.

Missy merely nodded, observing a dark shadow cross the young woman's face. She opted to change the subject. "So did Clem tell you that I'm going to be teaching in Shimmer Lake."

Alice managed a genuine smile. "That's good." She didn't know what else to say and her stomach swirled again. She sipped at her tea hoping it would calm.

"Yes, he wrote and they don't have a school out there. The homesteaders all educate their children at home. They've been trying to get a teacher for a few years but it's hard to get teachers who want to go west."

"But you don't mind?"

"Not at all. I see it as an adventure, a calling if you like. I feel like God brought me west. First to Craigstown so I could meet Clem and now He wants me on the frontier. The town plans to build a school and hopes it'll be ready by September when school starts."

"We're you from?"

"Boston."

Alice nodded. She'd never been to such a large city and she really couldn't imagine it. Craigstown had been too large for her liking and it wasn't nearly a city. "Is that where Clem is from, too?"

"No, he's from Chicago remember."

"Oh, yes. I think I remember. My brain seems to be all muddled these days." Both women looked up as the men walked up with poles over their shoulders and a string of fish.

"What do you think, Allie?" James smiled.

"Catfish?"

"I know they aren't your favorite but that's all we could get out here. We should catch whatever we can so our provisions last the duration."

"It's okay, catfish is fine. Missie and I have potatoes and beans ready to go with it. Sorry it isn't much but it's the best we could do under the circumstances." She gestured to the covered wagons nearby holding all their supplies.

"That sounds fine, Mrs. Cole." Clem smiled. "It's an adventure and it calls for adventurous meals too." His eyes twinkled. He was enjoying this 'excursion to the prairies' very much and saw each day as a new

55

opportunity. Roughing it in covered wagons didn't phase him at all, besides traveling slowly was better for Alice than the crowded train.

"How long do you think it'll take us?"

Clem took a seat next to Missy and kissed her forehead. He turned to look at Alice. "Bout three weeks, give or take."

"Probably give." Alice smirked. "I'm sorry the trip is so much slower because of me."

Missy smiled. "It's alright. We don't mind taking our time, it'll give us time to enjoy the landscape and get to know each other." She gripped Alice's hand. "I hope the trip isn't too hard on you, Mrs. Cole."

"Please, would you call me Alice." That made the lie a little easier to bear. Calling her Mrs. Cole just reminded her of the deception and the reason for it.

"Certainly. If you'll call me Missy."

"I'd like that." Alice gave her a smile. "Missy."

"We may be strangers for now, but I hope by the time we get there we'll be friends." The pretty young teacher grinned. "It's nice to at least know someone when you start in a new town. At least someone near my own age."

"I hope so, too."

"How old are you, Miss Branson?" James asked as he prepared the fish.

Alice took one look at what he was doing and her stomach churned she screwed up her nose, put her hand to her face and stood up, ran across the clearing and threw up behind a tree.

James grimaced. "It must be the smell of the fish."

Missy nodded. "Yes, my friend Harriet couldn't bare sharp smells when she was expecting."

"I better take it over yonder to clean up. She'll be fine once it's cooking. I just hope she can keep it down."

"Has she been very sick?" Missy's face was full of compassion.

"No, it's getting better now, since we got off the train four weeks ago. The doctor finally said she was ready to travel if we take it slowly."

"I hope she'll be okay. It can be hard going."

"I'll make sure she is. I better go and clean this somewhere else." He stood and smiled to Alice as she approached.

"I'm sorry." She grimaced at her brother.

"Don't be, Allie, I don't much like the smell myself. I'll be right back."

"Sure, I'll cook them once they are cleaned."

He smiled to her and grinned to Clem. "Ever cleaned a fish?"

Clem screwed up his nose. "That was the first time I ever even caught one."

"Come on, I'll teach ya."

Clem turned to smile to the two women. "Another new adventure." He leapt up to follow James.

Alice sat back down on the blanket. "They've become very good friends in a short time."

Missy smiled. "I'm glad. Clem doesn't have many friends because he's always moved around a lot."

"I'm glad too, and I'm certain you and I will be friends also."

Seven

Lane took a deep breath and knocked on the door to the gazette office. A muffled voice called "come".

Lane peered through the open door but didn't see anyone. He walked inside and the smell of ink hit him. He stood waiting for a moment in front of a wide desk.

"Sorry to keep you waiting, gotta get this week's edition out tonight and I had some last minute adjustments to make. What can I do for you, Mr?"

"Masters, the name is Lane Masters."

"Elliot Norris. You new to town?"

"Yes, just arrived yesterday."

"If you're wanting to put an advertisement in the paper I'm afraid it'll have to wait till next week's edition. I can't make any more adjustments, I'm just one man." Elliot swiped the black sleeve protector over his hot forehead. "I could really use some help."

"I'm not here to place an ad. I'm here to answer one."

Elliot raised his brows, he had no time to beat around the bush with this man, he had far too much to do.

Lane pulled the piece of paper out of his pocket and handed it to the man. "You're looking for a clerk?"

Elliot eyed him up and down. "You certainly look city bred, you educated."

"Harvard University, sir."

Elliot stroked his chin. "Any experience?"

"I worked on the paper at college."

"Well, I could really use the help and I haven't got time to be picky. Pay's two dollars a week plus a free subscription. Prove you're a hard worker and I'll raise it to three. Can't afford much more, I've only a small newspaper."

"When can I start?" Lane smiled.

"You know how to work a press?" Elliot tipped his head to the side.

"As a matter of fact I do. You need help?"

Elliot scoffed. "Most definitely. Come on, show me what you can do, Mr. Masters."

Lane nodded, and hurried around the desk to follow Elliot into the printing room.

＊　　＊　　＊　　＊

James stepped down from the wagon bed and looked back at his sister. "Are you sure you'll be alright, sharing with Missy?"

"I have to get used to not having you around all the time at some stage." She shuddered and turned the lamp up brighter. "And get used to the dark again."

James nodded. "If you're sure?"

"Where else would I sleep. Missy and Clem can't share a wagon it wouldn't be appropriate. I'll be alright, I won't be alone." She smiled at Missy as Clem approached with her and helped her up into the wagon.

James gave his sister another questioning look. Alice gave him a brave smile and nodded. "Goodnight, James."

He nodded. "We'll be just a few feet away and one of us will always be awake, just to keep an eye out."

Alice nodded again and moved the lantern closer to herself in the hope of staving off the clinging fear.

"Goodnight, Clem." Missy smiled and received his kiss.

"Night." He winked to her. "Goodnight, Alice."

"Goodnight, Clem." She wasn't entirely able to keep the tremble from her voice.

Missy dropped the flaps to enclose them in the wagon. Alice took a deep breath and bit her lips tightly together. She shuddered and let out a whimper she couldn't stop.

Missy looked at her. "Are you alright?"

Alice nodded and hoped Missy couldn't see the tears that threatened and the rapid pulsing in her temples.

"Are you sure? You look like you've seen a ghost."

"It's... it's... I... I just don't like the dark and being in unfamiliar places... I'm sorry. I will get used to it..." She flinched as the cry of coyote rang out through the still night.

Missy touched her arm and smiled. "It's just a coyote, it won't come near the wagon and the men are watching."

Alice smiled. "Sorry, you must me think me awful skittish. I'm seventeen years old, not a little girl."

Missy jerked her head back to look at Alice. "You're only seventeen?"

Alice smiled. "James and I are twins."

"You're awful young to be a widow already and with a child on the way." Missy squeezed her arm. "I'm so sorry."

"Thank you."

"It's alright, I promise you'll be okay here with me."

"Thank you, Missy. I'm sorry to be such a fraidy-cat."

"There's nothing to be sorry for, truly."

"Do you mind if we leave the lamp on, just on very low. I don't like it being completely dark."

"That's fine." Missy hastily put on her nightgown, wrapped a robe around herself and climbed under the covers of the large bed. It was surprisingly comfortable for a wagon in the wilderness. Clem had made it as comfortable as possible for the women. The other wagon was laden with their supplies so the men took bedrolls and slept near the fire just a few feet from the wagons. The four horses slept tethered on long ropes to the trees. Occasionally one would snort or paw at the ground.

The night noises were new to Clem and he had to admit to feeling a little vulnerable that first night out on the trail, sitting up in the darkness on his own. James slept propped up against the wagon wheel, his rifle across his lap.

Clem turned his head abruptly as an owl flew overhead and screeched. He let out a breath and clutched his rifle tighter. "Lord, please give me courage for this."

"Noooo, stoppp get off me... get off me." Alice screamed and lashed out at Missy, flailing her hands and feet.

Clem leapt up and headed for the wagon.

Missy sat up abruptly, moving away to avoid the hysterical woman.

James snorted awake immediately, jumped up and thrust open the flap of the wagon. He climbed up and gave Missy a sympathetic smile. Clem and Missy looked at each other. James crawled over to his sister and touched her back gently. "Alice. Allie, you're alright. You're safe."

She opened her eyes and heaved in breaths, her face full of terror. James lifted her up and held her in his arms until she calmed. He stroked her back and whispered. "You're safe, Allie, You're safe. I've got you. I'm here."

Alice sat back from him at last, her lips still trembling.

Missy had climbed down from the wagon and stood next to Clem in her robe.

James reached over to brighten the lamp. "Are you alright?"

"Yes. I'm sorry." Alice looked at Missy. "You moved near me and it gave me such a fright. I'm so sorry."

Missy gave her a sympathetic smile. "It's okay, Alice. I'm sorry I frightened you."

"It's not your fault... ohhh... I suppose she should know the truth. I can't promise this won't happen again."

"Truth?"

Alice nodded. "I should let you in on my secret."

Missy turned to Clem. "Do you know what she means?"

He nodded. "It wasn't for me to tell you. I gave Alice my word that I wouldn't and I won't. If she wants to tell you then good. I'm glad there'll be no secret's amongst us. But I will not speak a word of it. I promised."

Alice smiled and James gripped her arm. "Are you sure? I could talk to her if you like?"

"No." Alice's eyes flooded with tears. "I have to tell her. I need to face it." She blinked rapidly and sniffed. "I'll never heal if I can't face it."

"Heal?" Missy's voice was kind.

"Let's get some tea and I'll tell you. I doubt I'll sleep much tonight away."

"Come out by the fire, Allie, we can all talk out there. It may be more comfortable."

Allie gave her brother a smile and reached for her robe.

"Ohhhhhh. Alice." Tears rolled down Missy's cheeks. "Ohh, how terrible. I'm so sorry for you."

Alice leaned her head on James shoulder and he rubbed his hand up her arm. He hadn't stopped praying since she began talking, he was immensely proud of her for her courage. It was the first time she'd said the words aloud to anyone.

Clem put his arm around Missy and she sobbed into his shoulder. "How terrible, how can a man do that? How cruel, how terribly cruel."

Clem sucked back his own threatening tears as he thought of Lydia.

Missy calmed and sat up straight, she stood and walked over to kneel in front of Alice. Alice sat up and gave her a shy smile.

Missy put her arms out to embrace the younger woman. Alice smiled again and leaned into the hug. Missy gripped her tightly. "I promise to keep your secret as long as you want me to. Thank you for sharing it with me. I will do all I can for you and for the baby. I promise. You can rely on me." She sat back and looked Alice in the eye. "I'm so sorry Alice. I'm sorry I said I was happy for you. That must have been so horrible."

"You didn't know. You were being kind. It's what people say, and I have to get used to it." She placed her hand on her abdomen and sniffed. "This isn't what I planned for my life. I don't know what will happen going ahead, who I can trust and who I can't. If anyone will ever want me after this, if they know my shame, my disgrace...."

Clem dared to touch her arm. Alice looked up at him in the light of the fire.

"Alice. You speak of your disgrace, your shame? There is no shame. No disgrace. That evil man, he is the one who is the disgrace, he is the shameful one." Clem smiled at her and swiped away a tear of his own. "You are made stronger through your suffering."

James nodded. "I agree. There is no shame, Alice. Please know that. We don't look at you as a poor unfortunate woman who disgraced herself. We look

64

at you as a precious stone that has been chipped, and needs extra care and polishing to restore to an even brighter shine than before. Through this whole experience God will make you stronger and He will bless you. I'm not justifying the vile actions of a depraved man." He put his hand on his sister's stomach. "But here is a life growing inside you. One you never planned, or wanted. And as hard as it may be, this child is part of you. There is beauty in this brokenness, Allie." He kissed her forehead. "I pray you'll see it in time."

"I just don't seem to be able to get past the pain."

Missy touched her arm. "Hey, no one expects you to right away. I can't imagine the trauma you've suffered and all that is coming your way. But I want you to know that I will be by your side along with James and Clem, as long as you need me. I promise. You can count on us. Alright."

Alice's lip trembled and her eyes filled with tears. "Thank you." She managed. "Knowing I have allies makes all the difference to me. I feel like I could hope again." She put her hand on her abdomen. "I could even learn to love this child."

"Let's pray together, shall we?" Clem offered. The three others nodded and they bowed their heads and arm in arm they prayed for Alice and for the baby and that God would bring healing to her wounded heart and help her to trust again and to find hope and love.

"Amen." Alice lifted her eyes. She exhaled loudly and smiled to her new friends. "The Lord knew how much I would need you all. Thank you. I truly feel like I can carry on with the three of you by my side. No matter what happens or what people say."

"Brave girl." James kissed her hair. "Do you want to stay out here with me tonight by the fire?"

Missy gripped Alice's hand. "I'll fetch you a blanket, we'll both stay out here tonight."

Alice nodded.

James sat up against the tree trunk and stroked his sister's hair as she lay with her head in his lap. She seemed so small, so vulnerable, curled up in a blanket so trusting. It took him back to when they were children and they'd curl up in front of the fire like that and listen to their parents tell them stories from the Bible. Alice had always been his best friend, his confidant, and he couldn't imagine a better sister. Watching her suffer made his heart ache. He wished he could take it from her. He'd rather have ten gunshot wounds than see her suffer like this.

He leaned his head back against the rough bark and sighed. "Why did this happen to her, Lord Jesus?" He took a deep breath and felt the wound in his chest pull tight. "I don't understand. But I trust you. I'm going to need your help." He leaned forward and stroked her hair. "I promise to do everything I can for you, Allie. I'll defend you with my very life." He looked across at Clem and Missy, lying side by side asleep, Clem with hand on Missy's back. "Thank you for true friends, Lord Jesus. Thank you for prompting me to get Allie off the train in Craigstown and leading us to Clem. You are sovereign over everything, even the small details and I know you're with us. I know we can have a bright future with you to guide us." A gust of wind blew up, and James was sure he heard a whispered voice say, "fear not, for I am with you."

He smiled and stroked his sister's hair again as she slept.

Eight

Lane ran his forearm across his brow and stood up, put both hands to his back and stretched with a loud groan.

Elliot looked up and chuckled. "I know that feeling only too well."

"Phew, this newspaper caper is hard work."

"But rewarding."

Lane nodded. "I agree, it's a good paper. I really like this article about the new hotel. I think it's gonna be good for our town."

"Yes, Mr. Clementine has been out here a few times overseeing the progress. He's a good man. I think he has good intentions, he doesn't seem to be out to rip anyone off. I actually think it'll bring the good kind of prosperity to our town."

"I hope so." Lane bent over again and knocked the next row of type into place. "I really like it here. A man can forget the outside world even exists in a place like this."

"What is it you're trying to forget?"

Lane grimaced. "The war."

Elliot nodded but said no more. He scowled, struck a pen mark through a word and replaced it with the correct one. He looked up at Lane. "We'll I'm very glad you're here. Two weeks in and you're a good worker. I'm grateful to you."

"I'm grateful for the work, and the ability to forget." He stood up again. "There that page is set."

"Thanks, Lane, get a start on running it off and we'll do the final pages in the morning. I'm glad we have a week to print a paper. Can you imagine the daily papers. They must have a hundred people working presses non-stop to get them out."

Lane chuckled and lifted the plate to carefully slide into the press. "I can't imagine."

*　*　*　*

"Well, this is Shimmer Lake." Clem watched while the horses slurped at the cool water. "Through the trees and about twenty miles from here is the township." Clem's voice sounded proud as if it were his town.

"I'll be glad for a hot bath and a soft bed." Alice sighed and leaned back against the tree, glad to be still for even a short time. She rubbed her stomach and closed her eyes, fighting back the nausea. "I feel like we've been traveling for months."

"You and I have been on the road for more than a month, sister." James smiled and passed her the canteen. "Let's hope this is finally home for us."

Alice eagerly gulped down the water, she hadn't realized how thirsty she was until they stopped. She replaced the lid and passed it back to him, half full. "Home? I'm not sure what that is anymore. Our home on the farm didn't even feel like home anymore after... well... you know."

"I know, Allie. But this is our chance to start over. To put that behind us."

Alice's eyes glistened and her mouth twitched. "There will be no putting it behind me James. Not ever. What happened will always be a part of me. She rested her hand on her growing baby. "A part of us."

James sat beside her. "I know that, but you don't have to let it define who you become or shape your life."

"Don't you see, James? It has shaped my life. Completely upended my life and changed everything for me. If it weren't for what happened, Simeon and I would still be courting, you'd be on your way to college, Papa wouldn't be in jail and well..." she rubbed her stomach. "We wouldn't be here. I wouldn't be carrying a monster's baby." She shuddered. "So, while I know that I will heal and I can make the best of life, it will always have been a pivotal moment that shaped the course of my life."

James merely nodded. "The baby is innocent, Alice."

Alice looked at him. "I know that. Sometimes I picture myself with the baby in my arms and I'm overwhelmed with love but then he looks at me and all I can see is the face of Bluster Bill, smirking at me and I'm right back to resenting the baby again. I feel so conflicted."

Missy had been listening quietly and she approached the two as Clem re-hitched the horses. She sat down on the other side of Alice. "Of course you feel conflicted, Alice. The circumstances that have led you here are horrid, it's not fair that you have to carry and birth this child you had no say in creating." She gave her friend a compassionate smile and touched her arm. "No one expects you to act like this is a normal pregnancy and you're a delighted new mother to be. We understand that this will be hard for you."

Alice sniffed and smiled through gathering tears. "How do I not resent this child? For now while he or she is growing I can feel it inside of me and part of me wants to wrap the child up and protect it from the cruelty of its circumstances. But when it's born it'll be very different. I don't have a husband to celebrate a baby with and I'll be stuck with this daily reminder of how evil his or her father was."

"You could put the child up for adoption?" James touched her arm.

"I've thought about that. But then my mother-heart takes over and I can't help but thinking the child isn't to blame and they don't deserve a life in an orphanage or without someone to really love them." Alice's tears flowed then. "I just don't know how to feel. All children deserve to grow up loved and wanted and special and I don't know if can do that. Sometimes I wish I would lose the baby so that I didn't have to decide but then I'm horrified at my own thought. Now that the child exists, I couldn't bear to lose it." She shook her head. "I'm so confused."

James drew her into his arms and kissed her hair. "I know you are, Allie. And it's to be expected. This journey isn't going to be easy and I know that. But one thing you can count on is that I'll be there for you and for the baby, no matter what choice you make."

"Me too." Missy touched her back.

"And me." Clem joined them.

Alice nodded.

"Just remember what Papa said, the child is part of you, it's got your blood and it's got Papa's blood in its veins and that's what you need to remember. The baby is your flesh and blood and it's my flesh and blood and that there is a good reason to love the child."

"Let's just take it one day at a time, Allie. With God's help we'll make it. He will heal your wounded heart."

She nodded. "I'm glad you're with me, James. You give me the courage to face whatever is to come." She gestured to the trees before her.

James squeezed her arm. "I'm not going anywhere. I promise."

"And we're here for you too, Mrs. Cole." Missy smiled.

Alice reached over to embrace her. "Thank you, Missy, I was right, we've become the best of friends. I knew we would. And I'm glad you know the truth. I'm sorry for all the night terrors I've put you through."

"Don't be Alice. It's only been occasional and you haven't had them for four nights in a row now."

"I feel much stronger. I guess this time in the wilderness has been good for me. Although I've only been with three people I know and trust, it might be a different story when I'm amongst strangers."

"You'll do wonderfully, Alice." Clem smiled. "Now do you want to rest for a bit longer or just head into town?"

"Town, I think, there are warm beds and real chairs and tables, and maybe even a decent meal. I can't wait."

"I agree." James nodded. "Do you want to ride for a while?"

"Sure. My feet are awfully sore."

"Alright, hop up with me." James helped her up in the wagon and climbed up next to her. Missy joined Clem on the other wagon seat.

"Let's go home." The excitement was obvious in his voice.

"Home!" Alice smiled at her brother.

*   *   *   *

Lane woke from the nightmare drenched in sweat. He sat up and exhaled loudly. Swinging his legs over the side of the bed he stood to his feet. The nightmares hadn't stopped. In the last week he'd been awaken every night. Images of mangled bodies trampled under the hooves of advancing horses. Men crying out in agony, pleading for death. Surgeries done under horrific circumstances and often with no pain medication at all, it had been hard to come by in the primitive conditions he'd been expected to work in. He ran his fingers through his hair and paced back and forth in his room, trying desperately to free his mind from what he'd seen.

The darkness always brought the memories, he hadn't had a restful sleep since he'd left Virginia. It seemed these days whenever he closed his eyes he could see them.

Work was an adequate distraction but there was no such relief when he was sleeping. "Will I never be free of the war?" He struck a match and turned on the lamp shrugging into his clothes he left. It was close to four in the morning but there would be no more sleep for him. He might as well get an early start on printing the paper.

Elliot Norris strode in a few hours later. "Didn't expect to see you here so early?"

"Couldn't sleep so I thought I'd get a start."

"I can't pay you more for longer hours."

"I don't expect you to. Your wages are more than fair."

Elliot nodded as he slipped the black sleeve protectors over his clean white sleeves. "What's keeping you awake?"

Lane shrugged. "Just got a lot on my mind."

Elliot merely nodded.

"Work helps me keep my mind off it for a moment. I appreciate the distraction."

Elliot opened a copy of the gazette off the press to check the typesetting and layout. He looked at Lane. "The war?"

Lane nodded and crunched down the press twice as hard as normal. No more words were needed.

"Well, I appreciate your work, this issue looks good."

"Do you want me to do deliveries?"

"Jonah and Martin Stephenson usually come in after school, you know that."

"Sure. I'm just thinking of ways to be proactive."

"Keeping busy?" Elliot folded newspapers and placed them in a neat pile.

"Yeah."

"Sure, well the press needs cleaning, sadly I've been neglecting it a bit lately. Just been too busy to get to it."

"I'll get onto that as soon as I'm done here."

"It's a dirty job."

Lane shrugged. "I've done worse."

Nine

James pulled his wagon to a stop behind Clem's. He looked around. "its a pretty little town."

Alice nodded and gave him a brave smile. Clem and Missy were already climbing down from the wagon. James jumped down and walked around to lift his sister down. He made sure she was steady. "Are you alright?"

Alice nodded.

Clem and Missy joined them. "James, let's take the ladies to the café and we can take the wagon's out to the hotel and bed down the horses. They need a decent rub down and a rest."

"You have stables out there?"

"Yeah, I've employed a man to take care of the horses and carriages for the hotel."

"Will you be alright Alice?"

Alice sucked her lips in and blew out a breath. She squared her shoulders and looked at him with scared eyes.

"I'll stay with you, Alice." Missy smiled. "I promise."

Alice looked around nervously. She was going to have to get used to this sometime. James couldn't be with her twenty-four hours a day. She gave Missy a shy smile and nodded. "Alright."

James squeezed her arm. "Brave girl. We'll be as quick as possible. I promise. Then we'll get rooms at the boarding house and we can work out what we will do from there. I really should help Clem."

Alice nodded and took a deep breath.

Missy gripped her arm. "Come on, let's get some tea and a place for you to sit down out of the sun."

Alice gave her an uncertain smile and let herself be led.

They walked into the café and looked around. It was a sleepy little town and the café wasn't busy. Three men sat at one table and Alice felt her breath catch in her throat. Missy frowned and led her to the furthest corner, they sat down and a woman with a starched apron walked over to them.

"Hello." She smiled kindly. "You folks new to town?"

"Yes, Ma'am, I'm Missy Branson the new teacher?"

The woman smiled. "Oh, praise Jesus. We've been waitin' for a teacher. My young'ns are surely short of book learn'n"

Missy smiled. "I hope I can do you all justice, Mrs?"

"Agatha Jones, everyone just calls me Aggy."

"Aggy this is my friend Mrs. Alice Cole."

Aggy turned her eyes to Alice and observed her haunted eyes and her black clothing, rounding abdomen and tired smile. "Ma'am." She gave the young woman a sympathetic smile.

Alice managed to return her smile and then looked away.

Aggy took the pencil from behind her ear and slipped the notebook from her pocket. "So, what can I get you both?"

"I'll have coffee please and a muffin?"

Aggy jotted it down and swung her eyes to Alice. "Mrs. Cole?"

"Just toast with butter, please and chamomile tea if you have it."

"I do." Aggy frowned "I'll get it for you."

Alice nodded as the woman hurried away.

Just as Aggy left the room the three men stood from the table and placed coins on the table. They walked towards Alice and Missy. One of the men, a rough-looking, bearded man eyed Alice and clicked his tongue at her.

Alice took a deep breath and turned away from him, she began to shake and huddle in the corner. Missy stood and took the seat beside her.

The man scowled. "What's wrong with her?"

"She doesn't need men ogling her when she's just in a café." Missy put her arm around Alice.

"There ain't nothing wrong with a man appreciating a pretty lady." His voice was smarmy.

Alice shook again. Aggy walked in with their two cups. She noticed Alice's reaction and strode over, put the cups down and walked in front of the man. "Earl, just get out of here will ya."

The man sneered. "Fine, I'll go. That woman is crazy." He stormed out.

Alice sat up and Missy put her arm around her. "Are you alright?"

"Yes, sorry. He just frightened me." Alice took deep breaths.

Aggy sat down at the chair opposite and gave her a sympathetic look. "Has someone hurt you, dear?" The older woman asked.

Missy spoke. "Mrs. Cole recently lost her husband and it upsets her sometimes. He probably reminded her of the man who killed her husband."

Alice gave her a sad nod. She hated the deception but surely it was better than the truth.

"Well, I'm sorry, Mrs. Cole. Earl is pretty harmless really, he's just a bit uncouth. I'm sorry. Are you alright?"

Alice gave her a smile and nodded. "I will be." She turned when the door open and sighed with relief as Clem and James walked in.

They hurried over to the women. James looked at Alice's face. "Are you alright?" He turned to Missy. "What happened?"

Aggy hurried away to serve another customer.

"A man ogled her and made some suggestive actions. It just frightened her."

Missy stood and returned to her own seat with Clem next to her. James put his arm around Alice. "Are you alright?"

Alice nodded. "I'm sorry, I just over reacted. He looked like..." She shrugged.

James pulled her into his arms. "I'm sorry." He sat back and smiled.

"I'll be alright, I'll get used to it." She blinked away a tear.

"You're a brave girl, Alice."

Alice nodded to Clem. "I wouldn't be without you all. Thank you."

"You're welcome. Do you want to stay or would you rather leave?"

Aggy walked out with their food and placed it down. She nodded to the two men. She smiled at Clem. "Hello, Mr. Clementine it's good to see you again."

Clem grinned. "Aggy. How are you getting on?"

"As well as anyone, no complaints."

"I'm glad to hear it. This is my fiancée, Missy Branson."

Aggy raised her brows and nodded. She turned her eyes to James. He stood and nodded to her. "James Knight, Ma'am. Alice is my sister."

Aggy nodded. "Welcome to Shimmer Lake Township. Ya'll planning to stay?"

"We hope to." James gave his sister a smile. "Gotta find some land and a job."

"You're most welcome here. We're hard-working folk and we look after our own."

"Sounds like the town we need." James smiled and took his seat beside his sister again.

James finished his meal and wiped his face on the napkin. He placed it down on the table and turned to his sister. "Well, shall we find some temporary accommodation?"

Alice nodded to him.

"We'll come, too, we need to get rooms as well." Clem offered.

James tipped his head to him. "You aren't going to stay at your hotel?"

"It's not finished yet. We'll wait till it is complete and our quarters are ready, then we'll get married and move out there together." Clem squeezed Missy's hand. She smiled at him and they stood to join their friends.

*　　*　　*　　*

"I don't know if I want to be in a room by myself." Alice trembled as Mrs. Harvey showed them to rooms.

"I'll be right next door." James gestured to the room next to hers."

"But who will be across the hall?" She shuddered as she thought about it. "Men?"

"Yes, ma'am there is a young man in the room across from you. Works at the newspaper here. He's a kind man."

Alice shuddered. "I'll share with you, if you like?" Missy smiled. "I'd be happy to have a roommate. It'll be less lonely."

Alice lunged to hug her friend. "Thank you. That means the world to me."

"Of course." Missy clung to her. "It'll be fun."

Mrs. Harvey frowned slightly but shrugged. She eyed the young woman in her black clothing. She squinted. There was a hint of a pregnancy there, but it was nearly impossible to tell with all the layers. It was obvious the young woman had a story, but she wouldn't pry.

Clem turned to look at James. "Shall we share, too?"

James smiled. "If ya like, sure would be good to have company."

"Well, it's decided then." Clem turned to the woman. "I'll take care of the bill, ma'am, for all four."

James and Alice frowned and began to protest but Clem shook his head. "I'll hear no complaint. It's the least I can do."

Alice's stomach lurched and she put her hand to her mouth. "Ma'am. Where is the restroom?"

"End of the hall." The woman pointed out the door.

Alice hurried through the door. James gestured to Missy with his head and she nodded and followed.

The woman turned to James and Clem with a strange look on her face.

"Is ya sister, alright?"

"My sister, Mrs. Alice Cole, is in the family way, Ma'am. Just in her fifth month."

The woman nodded and her face curled up with sympathy. Her suspicions were correct. "Hopefully our town will have a doctor before she delivers."

"We hope so, too." James nodded kindly as the two women returned to the room. He smiled at Alice. "You two unpack, we'll be next door in our room."

Mrs. Harvey nodded.. "I'll leave you to it, supper is at seven in the dining room."

"Thank you, ma'am."

Clem touched Missy on the arm. "I'll go and fix the bill. See you at supper?"

Missy smiled and the two men followed the woman out.

Clem headed back to the room.

James was hanging his one good suit in the robe. He creased his eyebrows. "We can pay our way, Clem."

Clem nodded and folded his arm. "Brother, this is the least I can do, it was my idea that you both come here. I'd feel it an honor if you'd let me serve you."

James nodded. "Alright, but I promise to return the favor however I can."

"I'll take you up on that. I need to go out to the hotel and check on progress. Wanna come with me?"

James grimaced. "I should really stay around in case Alice needs me..." He looked up to see Alice and Missy standing in the doorway.

"I'll stay with her. I promise." Missy offered.

"I'll be alright. Missy was going to come with me to the library on the bottom floor. As long as she's with me I'll be alright. I have to get used to this sooner or later."

James gripped her arm. "You're a brave girl." He kissed her forehead. "We'll be back before supper, so you don't have to face it on your own."

"Thank you, you're a kind brother."

"My pleasure, Allie." James nodded to Clem and they followed the women down the hallway, saw them to the library and headed out.

Ten

Lane walked outside and took a deep breath. It was hot and stuffy in the printing office and he needed a breath of fresh air. He lifted his canteen to his mouth and took a long draft of the cool water. He leaned back against the wall and swiped his sleeve across his mouth to wipe away the drips.

He watched as two men walked out of the boarding house. One smartly dressed, the other looked like a farmer. Lane stood up and observed the shorter of the two men. His face looked familiar, but he couldn't recall why. He had the impression they'd crossed paths somewhere...

"Lane."

His bosses voice broke through his thoughts and he turned and walked back into the office to see what the man needed from him.

*   *   *   *

Alice stopped walking abruptly when they approached the dining room.

James touched her arm. "Come on, Allie. I'll make sure you're safe."

She looked around at the twelve other people sitting around the very large table, and shivered.

"Come on, there are four seats at the end." Missy encouraged her. "You can sit by me."

Alice nodded and tried not to make any eye-contact with the people around the table. She swallowed back her fear and took her seat next to Missy.

Mrs. Harvey gestured to the newcomers. "Mister Clementine, Miss Branson, Mr. Knight and Mrs. Cole." She introduced each person around the table.

As the eyes turned to her, Alice shuddered. *Come on Alice, you have to get over this irrational fear. These people aren't going to hurt you.* She took a deep breath and gave the people around her a brave smile.

The door opened and a man walked in. "Sorry, I'm late, we had a last minute amendment to the Gazette... his eyes swung to the new faces at the end of the table and his brows flew up. *It's her. The woman from the train.*

Alice lifted her eyes to him and her face revealed her recognition. The only seat left was across from her. Lane walked over and sat down. Alice leaned back and looked away from him. James squinted at the man, trying to work out how he knew him. He put his fork down and looked up at him. "You're the man from the train, the one who was kind to my sister."

Lane nodded. "Yeah." He put a piece of potato in his mouth and shrugged. Seeing her had a strange effect on him and his head began to swirl. *What's brought them to this town? Does anyone else know what happened to her? How's she getting on?* Thoughts and questions rumbled around his brain. He forced them into submission and smiled at Alice. "Name's Lane Masters."

"Hello, Mr. Masters. I'm James Knight, this is my sister Alice... ahhh Cole. Mrs. Alice Cole." He grimaced, but it seemed like Lane didn't notice the slip so he carried on. "This is my friend Clem and his fiancée Missy."

Lane nodded. *So, they're sticking with their ruse. I can't blame them.* He made small talk with the gentlemen while he ate but all the while he observed Alice. Her eyes darted from side to side like a scared puppy and she lowered her face anytime anyone tried to talk to her. She managed a few staggered words to him. *Poor woman, not yet eighteen and already so wounded.* His doctor's mind couldn't help but assess that she was looking pale and the way she pushed her food around it seemed she wasn't eating well.

Without thinking he reached across to touch her hand. Alice gasped and looked up at him with scared eyes. She snapped back her hand and her eyes filled with tears. She tried to hide the tremble to her lips.

"Sorry, ma'am. I didn't mean to frighten you. I was just going to ask if you're alright. You seem a little under the weather."

Alice gave him a shaky smile and forced herself to look at him. *Come on Alice, you can't recoil every time a man tries to be kind to you.* But it was involuntary. Her whole body would freeze up and that face would flash into her mind, Buster Bill with his foul-smelling breath and sinister smirk. She forced the image out of her mind and nodded to the man. "Sorry, Mr. Masters. You just gave me a fright. I'm alright."

Lane nodded. "Excuse me for asking, Mrs. Cole, but might I get you some tea?" He lowered his voice and smiled compassionately. "It'll help to settle your stomach."

Alice bit her trembling lips, there was something about the way he looked at her. It wasn't unkind but it was if he could see right through her and knew all about her. Strangely she felt herself relax and a voice in her soul whispered that he could be trusted. "I'm alright, thank you."

Lane raised his brows. "Well, I'm going to get some for myself so it would be no problem, ma'am."

She gave him a hesitant smile and nodded.

Lane smiled. "I'll be right back."

"I'll get that for you if you like?" Mrs. Harvey offered.

"No, ma'am. You stay here, I'll be right back." Lane stood up and hurried into the kitchen. Out of sight of the table he let out a loud groan. No matter how hard he tried to disregard his training, it would pop into his mind whether he liked it or not, threatening to make him face up to his past. He took a deep breath and sucked it back. "You're just a kind stranger helping out an unfortunate woman. That's all." He convinced himself and set about making the tea.

Alice looked up as Lane walked back in carrying a tray. He placed it on the table and sat down opposite her again. He gestured to a plate. "I brought you some toast, with just a skim of butter." He raised his brows.

Alice's face paled more. "Th... thank you." She managed. *Does he know about the baby? How could he?*

She pushed aside her supper and reached for the toast, it had been all she could keep down recently. She sipped at the tea and hoped Lane couldn't read her thoughts. *Even if he does know about the baby, he'd have no way of knowing about the baby's origins. I'm just a widow with a baby on the way.* She gave him a kind smile which he returned with a nod. She noticed he hadn't brought any tea for himself. *He's very kind.*

*　　*　　*　　*

Clem entered their shared room and slumped down on the bed.

James put down the book he was trying to read and looked over at his friend. "What's got up your nose?"

"The hotel."

"What about it? Yesterday you said the construction was coming on nicely."

"Yeah, it is, they're right on schedule for the start of next month."

"Then what is the problem?"

Clem sat up on the edge of the bed. "I thought I had a man lined up to be my groundskeeper and look after the stock and animals on the property but he's just got word that his father died, and his mother needs him so he's headed back east."

"Oh?" James said. "Surely you can find someone else."

Clem shook his head. "It was hard enough to find him. I don't have many people I trust, and he worked for me in Copper Hill."

"God'll provide the right man."

Clem nodded and looked up at his friend. Then a wide smile crossed his face.

James frowned at his sudden change of mood. "What is it?"

"Maybe He already has."

"What are you saying?"

"I'm saying, perhaps that's why the Lord brought you across my path."

"Me?"

"Yeah, you're a farmer, you're good with stock, you're honest, and I know you aren't going to leave anytime soon."

James' eyes grew wide. "You want me to look after your hotel?"

"The outside, the building, the property, gardens, stock, there'll be chickens, several cows, horses, other animals as we grow. Both for food and for entertainment for the guests."

"I wouldn't know the first thing about looking after a hotel."

Clem grinned. "I'm convinced you're the ideal man. I'd pay you well, and Hadley has a cottage out there on the property. It's less than a mile from town and it'd be ample for you and Alice."

"But I've got the money to buy some land. I was planning to farm." James shrugged.

"Then think of the hotel as a farm that needs to be taken care of."

James thought for a time. "Maybe. It does sound interesting. I'd have to talk to Allie though."

"Of course. Talk to your sister. But please tell me you'll consider it. You could start almost right away. Hadley'll be gone in a week."

James nodded. "I'll think on it overnight and pray about it." *Sounds like an intriguing prospect. It would be good for Allie to be close to town and friends. I worry about her being alone.*

* * * *

Lane lay awake and stared at the ceiling. Two things kept him awake, fear of the nightmares that haunted his sleep, and Alice. He couldn't work out why this particular woman had such a profound effect on him. He'd met women like her before. He'd seen far too many acts of such savagery during the war, as men from either side raided homes and took women as trophies.

He shuddered. War was so barbaric, and it had brought out the worst in so many men. He'd encountered good men too, but every day his hospital beds were filled with soldiers and civilians in horrible circumstances.

He shuddered as he thought about Margaret Waterston. The widow of one of the soldiers that had died on his watch. He remembered when the sergeant had gone to take the message to her and found her cowering in fear behind a shrub near her burned up homestead. One look at her and he knew what had happened. The sergeant had brought the terrified and beaten woman back to the hospital and it was there that Lane learned what had happened to her.

For her a child had also resulted from the attack, and they kept her in housing near the hospital to look after her. The sergeant felt she was his responsibility.

Lane sat up and leaned against the headboard. He lay his head back against the wall and let out a single sob. The woman wasn't nearly as brave as Alice, she seldom ventured out of her tent and was terrified whenever anyone came near. She learned to trust Lane and his nurses, but few other people could get close to her. A few weeks later the woman hemorrhaged badly and both she and the baby died. He shook his head.

He took a deep breath and looked out into the darkness of his room. "I won't let that happen to Alice." He said out loud, then he chastened himself. "Why do you care? You're not a doctor anymore? You can't do it." Just the thought of picking up a scalpel induced horrific images in his mind.

He sighed loudly. While he was working at the newspaper he could keep the dark thoughts at bay, even found himself laughing and enjoying life again. He'd almost allowed himself to forget, but here was this unfortunate woman and the darkness swirled again. He punched the mattress and slumped back down in his bed, pulled the covers over himself and turned over to face the wall, fighting to get control of his thoughts.

Eleven

Alice looked around the little cabin. "It's a bit gloomy."

"And sorely in need of a woman's touch." Clem gestured to the drab curtains and furniture.

"But it's cozy and we could make it our home in no time." James encouraged his sister.

Alice nodded. "Yes, I'm sure we could."

"So do you think we should take Clem up on his offer?"

Alice smiled. "I think it will be a wonderful opportunity for you and I'll feel better not having to eat with all those people every night. Every time they look at me, I'm sure they know." She instinctively put her hand on her abdomen, now beginning to show.

Clem gave her a smile. "No one knows, Alice. You are a widow expecting a baby."

Alice gave him a grateful smile. "Thank you."

"You don't think we are too far from town?" James asked her.

"Not at all." She turned to look out the window. "I can see town from here, we're less than a mile away."

"And on the edge of the hotel estate." Clem pointed out the side window to the large hotel and barn.

James turned to Clem. "I accept your job and this place."

Clem grinned and put his hand out to him. "That's wonderful. The Lord always provides the ideal people."

"He's answered my prayer for a good home for my sister." James gripped her arm.

Alice smiled at him and walked into the small kitchen and began opening cupboards.

Clem spoke up so they could both hear. "Make any changes you like to the house and bill it to the hotel."

"We couldn't do that. We can pay our way."

Clem fixed his eyes on James. "I insist. You're doing me a huge service by taking this job on, and I own this house. I want you to set it up the way you want it. I want it to be comfortable for Alice and for the baby."

Alice closed her eyes and hung her head. *Everyone expects me to keep this child. I'm not sure if I can...* She forced her mind to focus on the task before, checking out what the kitchen had available.

James nodded. "Alright."

"And your salary will be five dollars a week."

James eyes grew wide. "That's too much. Two dollars would be ample."

Clem frowned. "James, your job is essential, I can't run this place without you, and I see you being my right-hand man. It's only the wage you deserve and you have your sister and the baby to consider. It's only fair."

James squinted and screwed up his mouth then he looked at his friend and nodded. "I'll work hard for it. You can guarantee that."

"Very good. I'm excited about this." Clem turned to look at Alice. "Make a list of the changes you'd like to make, and I'll get my handyman onto it."

"I can do it myself." James furrowed his brows.

Clem grinned at James. "Of course you can. You're my handyman!"

James chuckled. "Of course."

"You have full access to the estate's horses, gigs and wagons. Help yourself when you need them. I give you all authority over all the grounds and maintenance of the property. You needn't come to me for permission. Just report back to me regularly."

"I will. I feel a bit overwhelmed by the trust you've placed in me. I hope I don't let you down."

"I'm not worried, the Lord led you to me and I'm certain you're the right man."

James merely nodded. "Well, I suppose I better go get our bags."

Alice's head flicked up. "I'm coming with you."

"Of course. Come on." James smiled and they followed Clem outside.

* * * *

James entered Clem's office and slumped into the chair. He exhaled loudly and swallowed twice. His dark eyes held a haunted expression.

Clem looked up from his ledger and put his pen down. "What's going on?"

James shrugged. "Never mind me, you wanted a report on the estate."

"James, the report can wait. You're doing a great job here. In just a month you've got this place looking and running great. I'm confident we're on schedule for our opening."

James nodded.

"So, forget the report. There's something on your mind."

James nodded again and dropped his head. He reached into his pocket and pulled out a telegram. He passed it across the desk to Clem.

Clem frowned and took it, opened the envelope and slipped out the card. He read the short message and closed his eyes and shook his head. "I'm so sorry."

James scratched his chin and sniffed. "I knew it was coming, but I wasn't ready for the emotion it would bring." He swiped his sleeve across his eyes.

"Does your sister know?"

James closed his eyes and shook his head. "I can't add to her troubles. She already blames herself for Pa being in prison. Now that he's been executed, she'll only take it personally." He shuddered. Saying the words out loud made it even more real.

"She knew it was going to happen didn't she?"

"Yeah."

"Then she deserves to know."

"He wrote a letter a week ago saying his goodbyes and telling her not to blame herself. He doesn't regret making sure that man could never hurt another person."

"I imagine many men would do the same."

James nodded and scratched his chin again. He grimaced. "I'm not sure I could kill a man in cold blood, even if it was my daughter he'd hurt."

"You don't think he deserved it?"

James snapped his head up to look at his friend. "Bluster Bill definitely deserved to be punished for what he did, but I think it should be left to the law. It's one thing to defend yourself but to kill outright? I'm not so sure I could. I'm glad he's not able to hurt another woman and I think he deserved the death penalty, but I'm not sure I agree with Pa's choice."

"I can understand his anger." Clem raised his brows. "If it were my daughter or my wife, I think it would cross my mind."

"Don't get me wrong, Clem, I've certainly been through all the emotions, and I've struggled with hate because of what that man did to my sister. I've also struggled with overwhelming guilt." He sighed and toyed with his hat in his lap.

"Guilt?"

"I walked in on them, tried to get to her but he shot me twice. I lay there bleeding out unable to help but I heard everything." He closed his eyes and shuddered. "I'll always have to live with that. Knowing I was there and couldn't stop what was happening to her."

"Does she blame you?"

"No, she's done nothing but thank me for my care of her."

"She knows how close you came to dying. I'm glad you survived or she'd've been left with no one."

James nodded. "Thanks, Clem. I'm thankful for an understanding friend. My biggest fear is that Alice would be ostracized. It's not fair that she gets punished for what he did to her. Why does this world shun women like her when she's done nothing wrong. I've heard men say they're 'ruined' or 'soiled.' Like somehow they brought it on themselves. It's so cruel. If she was truly a widow no one would think that at all."

"There's none so queer as folk they say." Clem shrugged. "I don't get it either, but I know it's how Lydia felt. She was sure I'd feel that way about her especially when she found out about the baby. She couldn't bear to live with the shame. Even though I never felt that way. There was no shame to me, just a wounded heart that needed tender care." Clem sucked in a breath fighting the threatening tears.

James nodded. "I agree."

"Alice'll find a good man. There are men who feel the same as we do and won't hold it against her."

"She doesn't like having to lie."

"I know, and I'm confident she won't have to forever."

James nodded and they both grew silent for a time.

"I think you need to tell her about your pa. She deserves to know."

James scratched his chin. "Yeah, I know."

"Go and talk to her now."

"What about the report?"

"No need. You're doing a fine job, the hotel grounds are looking great. I'm glad I employed you."

"Thank you. You've been most kind."

"Least I can do."

"So have you set a wedding date?"

Clem grinned. "September first. A week after the opening of the hotel. Our wing will be ready by then."

"When does she start school?"

"September twelfth I believe. Give us a week or so to get used to each other before school starts. I hope you'll both come to the wedding."

"I will, for certain. Alice will have to make that choice for herself. She'll be nearly eight months along then."

"We'll understand if she doesn't want to come. I hope she will though. I know Alice means a lot to Missy."

"Allie has been very grateful for Missy's support. She's glad that the two people who 'know' besides me, love her anyway."

Clem raised his brows and frowned. "We don't love her 'anyway'. We love her. The circumstances of her life are inconsequential."

James gave his friend a sideways smile. "Thank you." There were no other words needed. He stood, nodded to Clem and left the room.

*   *   *   *

Alice sucked in a breath when the door opened. It still made her recoil. She spun on her heals to look at the door. She released her breath. "Hi, James."

"Sis." He gave her a sad smile and turned to remove his hat and boots.

"What brings you home in the middle of the day? Did I not send you with enough food?"

"No, Allie, it was ample as always, thank you. I came home because I need to talk to you about something."

The deep furrow to his brow and the shadows across his eyes made fear rise in her heart. She strode out of the kitchen. "What is it?"

"Got any coffee?" He smiled as he sat down on the small sofa.

"Sure." Alice returned with two cups of coffee and a plate of cookies. She took the seat next to him and passed him a cup. "What is it?"

James took a long draft of the coffee as though seeking comfort from it. He placed it back on the small table, took a deep breath and reached for her hand. "I got a telegram today?"

"A telegram? From whom?"

"Doctor Reynolds."

Alice sat back and frowned. "From Virginia?"

James nodded.

"But why would he send you a telegram?"

James closed his eyes and sighed. He slipped his hand in his pocket and passed it to her.

Alice read the telegram and put a hand to her mouth and tears ran down her cheeks. She dropped the note and lifted both hands to her face and sobbed. "Papa, o Papa, I'm so sorry, I'm so sorry."

James wrapped her in his arms and rocked as he held her. He leaned his head against hers and his own tears came.

It was some time before Alice regained her composure, sat back from her brother and dried her eyes. She dropped her head to her chest. "I'm sorry, James." Her lips trembled.

James tipped his head to the side and reached out to lift her chin. "Why are you sorry?"

Alice sniffed. "Papa is dead because of me." She sucked in her lips and her eyes flooded with tears again.

James lifted a hand to each cheek and leaned forward to kiss her forehead. He fixed his determined eyes on hers. "Allie, darling, he's not dead because of you. It's because of the choice that evil man made. Papa told me he'd give his life for you a hundred times over, and so would I. Please, don't feel any guilt for this. You've suffered enough. I would give my life to take this from you." James paused and swallowed, then exhaled a deep breath. "I couldn't that day, and I can't now. But I can be here for you and do everything I can to see you happy and loved." He smiled then and brushed her cheek. "That's what I want for you. Oh, Allie, you're my favorite sister."

That brought a smile to her face. "I'm your only sister."

James nodded. "And the only family I have in the entire world. "You and the baby." He raised his brows.

Alice placed her hand on her growing baby and gave him a shaky smile. "I feel so mixed up about the baby."

"What do you mean?"

"Yesterday, I felt it kick and waves of love washed over me, and I pictured myself rocking him in the cradle. Then I saw the baby's face and it was that man's face and I felt such a sense of revulsion and anger towards the baby." A tear streaked down her cheek. "How could I ever feel that way about an innocent child."

"It's not the child you feel that way about, it's the evil man."

"But the child is part of that man, he always will be. I'll forever see his face in the child."

"You've forgotten one very important thing, Sister."

She tipped her to the side in question.

"That child is part of you, it's part of me, it's part of Papa and Mama."

Allie nodded. "I know. And I want to love this child, for that reason, and because it's innocent, no matter how it came to be." She sighed and rubbed her abdomen again. "But what if it does look like it's father."

"Father?" James raised his brows. "That man isn't your child's father."

"What are you saying?" Allie tipped her head to side.

"He may have provided the seed, but that does not make him a father. I'm confident this child will have a father some day, a man who is fiercely in love with you and that the child will grow up just like his father in looks and mannerisms – like the man who raises him or her. Remember when the Bradley family adopted those two little girls and as they grew they were so much like their adopted parents."

Alice nodded. "Mama always said that nurture is just as important as nature. I'm not sure I really understood what that means."

"It means your origins have little to do with how you turn out. We didn't turn out the way we are because of who our parents were, we turned out this way because of who our parents raised us to be. The Bradley twins were the product of a liaison with a saloon girl, remember, there was a huge scandal and the mother died in childbirth and no one wanted to take on the children of a 'loose woman' but the Bradley's had mercy on them and now they are wonderful grown, Christ-fearing women. Chrissy is engaged to the pastor's son."

Alice smiled. "I remember, Chrissy was my friend."

James leaned forward and lay his hand on his top of his sister's still resting where her baby grew. "And this child will be the same. What's required isn't good parentage but good loving parenting. Show this child that no matter their origins they're special, loved and wanted. That God has a plan for them."

Alice put her arms out to embrace James and he leaned forward to reciprocate.

"Thanks, James, I needed to hear that. I know it will be hard but you're right." She sat back from him. "Will you remind me of that often. Help me to love this baby." Her face lit up and she gasped. "Ohhhhhh." She gripped her brother's hand and held it to her stomach.

James grinned. "What is that?"

"He's kicking and moving about in there." Alice's eyes lit up, her mother heart responding to the growing child. "Ohhhhh."

"Wow." James continued to feel it. "He's active alright. A lively one." He pulled his hand back.

"I hope he grows up to be just like his uncle James."

James nodded. "You know we ought to stop referring to the baby as he, it could just as easily be a girl."

Alice nodded. "That's true. I suppose one of these days I'm going to have to think about names."

James gulped and reached up to brush away a tear.

"What is it?" Alice gripped her brother's hand.

He smiled kindly and squeezed her hand. "That's the first time you've talked about naming the baby. It sounds like you've decided to raise him or her after all."

Alice bit her lip and shrugged. "I still don't know, James, it'd be awful hard to give it up after growing inside me for so long. But part of me doesn't know if I could bear to raise the child. Especially all alone."

James gripped her hand again. "You'll never be alone, Allie. I promise you that."

"You'll marry someday, James, you won't want the burden of your poor unfortunate sister and a baby."

"Allie, stop that. You aren't a burden and you aren't unfortunate. You're my priority now, I won't marry until I know you're cared for and happy."

"I couldn't be the reason you don't get to have a family..."

James lifted his hand to her. "Hush. You're my family, and I love you, Alice Knight." He grimaced. "Alice Cole. And that's all we'll hear about that. You are my priority, you and the baby. Alright. It's what I want."

"Thank you, James." She smiled again. "You know if the baby turns out to be a boy I think James would be a wonderful name."

James frowned. "Wouldn't that be a bit confusing?"

"We could call him Jimmy, or Jamie or Jim, there's lot's of options."

James nodded and kissed her forehead. "Of course."

"Now, I must get on with the wash."

James helped her to her feet "You've got this place looking great, Sis. A real little home."

"I like it here. I feel safe here."

"I'm so glad."

"Will you still take me to town this afternoon so I can go to the store."

"Of course." He winked and hurried out the door.

Twelve

"Oh, where is he? He's more than an hour late." Alice scowled at the clock. She took a deep breath. "Well, you're going to have to get used to going to town on your own sooner or later, Alice. Might as well be sooner." She forced down the tremble in her voice and prayed for the Lord's guidance.

Determinedly she snatched her shawl from the hook, scooped up her basket and opened the door. She bit her lips to keep them from trembling and stepped outside, swung her eyes towards town and took another deep breath.

Closing the door firmly behind her she took another deep breath and set her chin. "Lord, be with me." She prayed as she took the first few hesitant steps.

A butterfly fluttered up to her and landed on her basket. She paused to watch it flap it's wings a few times and then it flew away. She smiled. The little creature was so vulnerable yet so beautiful and it gave her courage.

As she walked she thought about her conversation with James. Laying her free hand on her baby she spoke aloud. "I want to love you. Please, Lord, show me how to love this child." She thought about her father. Pushing all the guilt from her mind she focused on the wonderful memories from her childhood.

She was daydreaming so much she didn't notice the man step out of the Gazette office. "Woah, there." He put his hand out to her.

"Noooo." Alice cried out and covered her face, cowering instinctively.

"Hey, Mrs. Cole. You're alright."

Alice looked up at Lane and shuddered. *Come on, Alice, you can't freak out every time someone startles you.*

He dared to touch her arm and felt her recoil, but she didn't pull away from him. "I'm sorry, I frightened you, I just didn't want to bump into you. You seemed so far away."

"Sorry. I just..." She shrugged, how did she explain her reactions to someone who didn't know her story.

Lane gave her a kind smile. "It's quite okay, Mrs. Cole. Are you alright?"

Alice exhaled loudly and gave him a determined smile. "Yes, thank you, Mr. Masters. I was just daydreaming."

He nodded. "Where are you headed?"

"I thought it was high time I was brave and went to the store on my own." She blushed. "You may think that's foolish, that I don't like to be on my own."

"I don't think it's foolish. You're in a new place, where you don't know many people. You've seen some tough times, and I imagine it's not easy. I know a thing a two about that, 'course me, I prefer to be alone most of the time."

"Really?" She eyed him. "You seem so social."

Lane smirked. "I'm good at fitting in when I need to, and sometimes company's good when I'm trying to avoid my thoughts."

"I know what you mean." For a reason she couldn't place, she felt comfortable with Lane. There was a deep sadness in his eyes, but a kindness too. She instinctively knew he'd never hurt her. In a way he was like Clem, only with a shadow hanging over him. *I wonder what he's seen that has caused that. Perhaps we are both wounded souls.*

"Would you allow me to carry your basket for you while you shop, Ma'am? It might get heavy and well, with your condition and all..." He gestured to her rounding figure.

"Ummmm," Alice stammered. Her mind said 'flee, run, get away', but something in her heart whispered, "*It's alright, you can trust this man.*" It was an unusual feeling to have such an instinct about someone she barely knew. *Perhaps I'm healing after all.* He was still waiting for her answer. "Ummm. That would be kind." She took another deep breath, quite unable to believe she was being so brave.

There was something about Alice that drew Lane. She had a sweet vulnerability about her, and he knew her soul was wounded, much like his was, perhaps that was it. He reached out for her basket and she handed it over. Lane gestured toward the store.

*   *   *   *

"Whoa, Roger." James hauled the Clydesdale to a stop, grateful for the strength of the horse as he dragged the large log into place. He slapped the horse on the neck. "Good boy." Unlinking the log from the chain he stood and stretched his back. It was the last log and it almost completed the circle of logs around the fire pit he'd built in the middle. A fireside meeting place for people from the hotel to relax in the long summer evenings. "All right, let's get you unhitched." He loosened the yoke and led the horse back towards the barn.

Just as he closed the gate on the horse something occurred to him. "Oh." He yanked his pocket watch from his pocket and grimaced. "Oh no. Alice."

He thrust the yoke over the hook, he could clean it later, she needed him. Yanking his coat from the hook by the door he sprinted for the cabin. Hurrying in he was dismayed to not find her there. Taking a deep breath to stave off the panic he looked around. Her shawl and basket were missing. "She went by herself." He smiled. "Lord, watch over her."

Taking off at a sprint he headed for town to find his sister. He didn't get far, when he spotted Lane and Alice walking toward him, Lane had Alice's full basket on his arm. He smiled and approached them. "Hello."

Lane gave him a nod. "Mr. Knight. I offered to carry your sister's basket home for her, she ought not be lifting too much in her condition." His voice was kind.

James gave his sister a nod. "Thank you, Mr. Masters, I'm much obliged." He reached for the basket to carry it. "Sorry, I was late, Allie. The job took a lot longer than I thought."

Alice smiled. "It's alright, James. I have to do this on my own sooner or later. I'm never going to get over my fears if I hide in the cabin all day. Mr. Masters was kind enough to help me."

James shook his head. "I'm proud of you, Alice."

She blushed and shrugged. "He seems pretty harmless to me."

"I am. I can assure you that." Lane smiled. "It's my pleasure. I enjoyed the conversation too, Mrs. Cole."

Alice groaned internally. "Mr. Masters, would it be too forward to ask you to call me Alice? I prefer it to Mrs. Cole." *It's a lie!* She stifled a sigh.

"It's not too forward. I'd like that, Alice, that's a pretty name, and in return I'd like it if you'd call me Lane. Mr. Masters feels much too formal."

"Very well, Lane."

"I'll leave you to it. I must get back to the gazette."

Alice nodded. "It's a very fine newspaper, my brother and I enjoy reading it."

"Yes. It is," was all Lane said. "Take care of yourself, Alice."

"Thank you, you too, Lane."

Lane nodded and hurried back to town.

James stood looking at his sister with his brows raised.

"What?"

"I never expected to see you walking along with a man, seeming so calm."

"I'm not so calm on the inside. But he seems to be very kind, and I don't know." She shrugged. "He makes me feel safe, kinda like Clem."

James put his arm around her and they walked to the house. "I'm so glad, it means you're healing Allie, I can't believe you went to town by yourself."

"I wasn't by myself, God was with me. I have to learn to be brave again. I can't carry on with life seeing every man as a monster who's waiting to hurt me. There are good men in this world, and they by far outnumber the bad. I'm shaking on the inside but I have to do this, if I ever hope to have a good life."

James opened the door for her and placed down her basket. He turned and drew her into an embrace. Kissing her hair he whispered. "Praise God. I'm so pleased."

*   *   *   *

Lane yanked a piece of paper from the press, wadded it up and fired it at the overflowing wastepaper basket in the corner.

Elliot looked up from his desk and scowled. "You're wasting a lot of paper today, Lad."

"Sorry." Lane reached for another page and started over.

"Something on your mind."

Lane nodded and said nothing else.

Elliot raised a brow, shrugged and went back to work. "Ain't none of my business, just see to it you don't cost me too much in wasted paper or I'll take it out of your wages."

"Yes sir." Lane sighed. He forced his mind to focus on the task, but it kept wandering to Alice. Her eyes seemed so full of hope for the first time. He knew she was beginning to overcome the ordeal that had taken place. Oh, of course she had a long way to go but she was brave and courageously facing up to it slowly and finding peace again. Lane grimaced as he ran the page through the machine. *I wish I had her courage. I'm too scared to even close my eyes. I can walk away from my past and never have to go back, but she'll have to live with the child as a constant reminder, yet she seemed so bright today. What was it she said, 'the Lord sustains us.' Hmmmmpf.* Lane shrugged and fed in another pile of paper. *He never sustained me, God's so far away. He's forsaken me.*

As clearly as if he'd stood in the same room Lane heard a voice in his soul say "It was not me that walked away." Lane sucked in a breath and nodded, forcing his mind to focus on the paper and away from his own hurt and shame.

Thirteen

"I'm exhausted." Alice yawned as James helped her up the stairs.

"I'm not surprised, that was a long day."

"But so worth it. I'm glad the hotel is officially open. A testament to all your hard work."

"Oh, it's Clem's work, I'm just the groundsman."

"But the grounds look wonderful." Alice gestured to the coffeepot.

James nodded. "You sit, I'll get the coffee." He hurried back with two cups of hot coffee and slipped into the seat opposite her.

Alice took a long sip of the coffee and smiled. "It's wonderful that Clem invited the townsfolk to have a free night at the hotel."

"Yes, a sort of 'trial run' for it. He says it's as much the towns hotel as his and he wants the folk to be supportive."

"Even Mrs. Harvey seemed delighted."

"Yes, Clem is determined he won't be competition. The boarding house will always be needed, for long term tenants and those who can't afford the hotel."

"I hope he brings the right sort of prosperity to the town."

"Me too." James drained his cup and squinted at her. "I saw you chatting to Mr. Masters again. Is he becoming a friend?"

Alice scowled. "Not in the way you're implying, James Knight. He was just inquiring after my health. He asked me how far along I was."

"He seems very interested in you."

"He's just being kind. He hasn't lived in town long and doesn't know many people."

James nodded. "Well, I'm glad you have a friend. You deserve to be happy."

"James, I don't need you meddling. You know as well as I do that as soon as a man finds out the truth about me that'll be the end of it. Friendship is all I require and he must never know."

"Alright, Alice. But don't deprive yourself of happiness if a man is interested."

"How could that be possible? I could never marry a man in such a lie, and yet if I told the truth he'd never want me, so it's just best I stay as I am."

James sighed. *Lord, help her to see she is worthy of love and bring along a man who will know the truth and still love her and the baby*

Alice changed the subject. "I can't wait for next week. Missy and Clem are finally getting married."

"Yes, I'm happy for them both."

"He asked you to be his best man, I'm so delighted."

"And Missy asked you."

"I just hope I can stay on my feet. I'm nearly eight months along and I'm getting very tired quickly these days."

"God will sustain you."

"Yes, He will. Now I must get some sleep. I have to help Missy this week with the wedding set up. I'm so glad for that beautiful wooded glade out by the pond that you've helped to clear. It's a beautiful spot for an intimate wedding."

James took the cups back to the kitchen and helped Alice out of her chair.

* * * *

"Oh, Missy, you look so beautiful." Alice gushed.

Missy turned from side to side and watched her dress sway in the mirror. "I can't believe I'm getting married today."

Alice put her arm around her friend, and they leaned their heads together. "It's so wonderful. Clem is a good man."

"I know. I love him so much. You'll find a man like him one day, I know it."

Alice stood back and gave her friend a shy smile. "You're kind to say that, but I'm not so sure it'll happen. But today is about you. Are you ready?"

"Yes. I'm so glad you're with me."

"I hope I can stay on my feet, and I hope the weather stays good."

"I hope so, too. Clem said he thinks we'll get an early winter. I hope not, it may delay the start of school."

Alice merely nodded and rubbed her stomach. The baby was particularly active that day. She winced.

Missy caught the gesture. "Are you alright?" She squeezed her friend's arm.

"Yes." Alice gave her a wide smile. "The baby is just making himself known today. But I'm looking forward to your wedding. Come on, your groom is waiting. James is parked out front ready for us."

Missy gushed and the two women walked to the door. James jumped down from the carriage and carefully helped both women up. He picked up his sister's wince and frowned. Alice flashed him a look to reassure him she was fine. She wouldn't ruin their day. James gave her an uncertain nod but vowed to keep an eye on her and as soon as possible he'd insist she get off her feet.

*　　*　　*　　*

James sat his sister at the café table and she sighed with relief as she sat down. She flashed him a grateful smile.

"Chamomile tea?"

"Yes, thank you. And toast with butter?"

James put his hand on Alice's shoulder. "Sure."

Clem sat his new wife opposite Alice, kissed her cheek and hurried to follow James.

Missy put his hand out to grip Alice's. "Are you alright?"

"Yes, I just need to rest for a time."

Missy grimaced. "I'm sorry, you've been on your feet all morning."

Alice gave her a kind smile. "I wanted to be there for you. It was a beautiful wedding."

"Yes, simple and perfect, just the way we wanted it. We didn't want a big party or fanfare, just our dear friends and an intimate ceremony."

"It was perfect and I'm so glad I got to be there for you. I can rest while you're away."

"Make sure you do. You need to look after yourself and the baby."

"I will."

James sat down and passed his sister a cup and placed his own in front of him.

Alice gave him a grateful smile. He nodded and turned to join the conversation.

Clem took the seat opposite him, next to his new bride. He passed her a cup and sat his own down. "Thanks for joining us for lunch. I know it's not the traditional wedding breakfast." Clem shrugged and raised his brows at Missy.

Missy smiled and gripped his hand. "It's what I wanted. I prefer small and intimate, than sharing this with lots of people I don't know. The church-folk already celebrated with us this morning at the service."

"I'm very glad to be here with you." Alice smiled.

Clem looked over. "We want to thank the both of you for being such good friends. Your lunch is on us today."

"That's not necessary..." James began to protest.

Clem frowned. "It is the least we can do. You'll be taking care of the hotel for a week while we are off on our honeymoon."

James nodded and frowned. "That's a big responsibility. I'm not sure I'm up to it."

"Of course you are. The staff know how to run it, you'll just oversee."

"I'll do my best." James looked up as Agatha placed the plates before them.

Clem gave her a grateful nod. "I appreciate you opening up for us on a Sunday."

"My pleasure – it's for a worthy cause."

"Well, we appreciate it." Missy smiled.

Agatha nodded and hurried away.

"Are you looking forward to going on your honeymoon?" James asked.

"Yes." Missy smiled. "I've never been to Chicago."

Clem nodded. "My father can't wait to meet you."

Missy cringed. "I hope he's not disappointed in me."

"Not possible." Clem kissed her cheek. "He'll adore you. So will my brother and sister."

"Thank you."

James and Alice smiled at each other.

They ate together and chatted happily until the clock on the bank struck two. Clem smiled and gripped Missy's hand. "It's time to go, we have a train to catch, darling."

Missy grinned. "I can't wait."

The group stood and walked together to the stage platform. The luggage already sat atop the waiting stage. Missy embraced Alice. "Please take care of yourself. I'll see you in a week."

"Thank you, Mrs. Clementine. I will."

Missy stood back and grinned. "Mrs. Clementine. That sounds so wonderful."

"I'm so pleased for you."

"Come on, Missy." Clem put his hand out to her. She nodded and allowed him to help her up into the stage.

"Goodbye." He offered with a wide smile and climbed up next to his bride.

The siblings watched as the stage drove away. Alice placed her hands on her stomach and sighed loudly. James turned to her and gripped her arm. "Allie, are you okay?"

"I'm just tired."

"Stay here, I'll get the carriage." He gestured to the seat.

"I'm okay, James. I can walk to the livery."

"Alice... You need to rest."

"I don't want to be here alone." She looked around, the old fears beginning to grow.

James shrugged. "I can't ask you to walk that far. You're almost eight months pregnant and you've been on your feet all morning..."

"Good day, you two." A cheery voice broke through James' words.

"Good day Mr. Masters." Alice smiled. She was becoming comfortable with him. "Just out for a walk?"

"Yeah, I've been cooped up inside all week trying to get the paper out, sometimes I just like to take a walk in the fresh air, to clear my head."

James nodded. "Mr. Masters could wait with you Allie?"

Lane frowned and looked from face to face.

"I don't need babysitting!" Alice groaned.

"Allie. You can't walk that far, and you don't want to stay here alone. I know you trust Mr. Masters, if he'd be willing to wait with you, I can get the carriage and get you home."

Lane smiled. "I'd be happy to."

Alice began to protest but the look of frustration in her brother's eye made her stop. She looked up at Lane and nodded. "Alright."

Lane nodded. "Let's sit down over there." He gestured to the seat under the wide awning.

James flashed Lane a grateful smile. "Thank you, Mr. Masters, I won't be long."

"Lane. Please. And take your time. Your sister will be quite safe, I promise."

James nodded and turned to hurry up the street. Lane gestured to the seat. "Come on, you need to get off your feet." He dared to touch her arm.

Alice smiled, surprised she didn't feel herself recoil. "Thank you," she said as she allowed him to lead her. Relieved to know that she could actually allow herself to trust a man who wasn't her brother.

Lane seated Alice and she leaned her head back against the wall and sighed loudly. He took a seat next to her and gently touched her arm. "How are you feeling?"

"Hot and tired, a little sore if I'm honest." She sat up and gave him a brave smile.

"Do you want me to find you some water?"

"No, thank you. I'll be home soon and I can rest. It's been a long day."

"Make sure you take it easy, Alice. You need to rest for the baby and for yourself. It's important you're strong." Lane grimaced and scolded himself again.

Why can't I stop from sounding like a doctor? What is it about this woman that brings this out in me. I'm determined I'll never practice medicine again. But if he was honest that resolve was crumbling. It was Alice, she had a profound effect on him and almost made him wish he could return to practicing medicine. There was something vulnerable and trusting and needy about her, that was what he'd loved. He felt that longing raise its head again. The one he'd felt when he'd entered medical college. The longing to help the innocent, the broken, the hurting, the sick, to bring relief to them and to see them thrive. The very longing the war had forced out of him. He sighed without meaning to.

Alice frowned and tipped her head. "Why do you care so much anyway? You seem very knowledgeable about pregnancy."

"Um... I ah..." he shrugged. "Just know a thing or two or pregnancy, I've been present... for a few births."

"Really?"

Lane nodded and exhaled in relief when James came around the corner with the wagon. Lane stood and helped Alice from the seat. He lifted her by the waist up into the wagon next to James who took her hand and helped her up. "Much obliged to you, Lane."

"It's my pleasure. Your sister's good company."

"Thank you, Lane." Alice smiled.

"See to it she puts her feet up for the rest of the day and gets plenty of rest and good nutrition." He heard himself say.

"I will." James nodded. "Good day."

"Good day." Lane tipped his head, turned on his heels and strode towards the Gazette office.

James turned to Alice. "Are you alright?"

"I will be when I can put my feet up."

"How did you feel being alone with Lane?"

Alice smiled. "I feel safe with him."

"I'm glad to hear it."

"I can't quite place it, but there is something about him."

"Oh?" James raised his brows and gave her a knowing grin.

"Nothing like that, James Knight. I'm not sure I'll ever be able to have a real relationship with a man."

"So, what is it then?"

"I don't know, he seems nurturing some how."

"He cares, I suppose."

"Yes, I know, but it's not like with you or Clem, you both care, but Lane is different. Like he seems to know instinctively what I feel and how to help. There's a darkness about him, like he's suffered somehow, but it seems nurturing and kindness come naturally to him and for a moment when he's caring about me it seems like he forgets the darkness and focuses on me."

"What are you suggesting?"

"I really don't know. Perhaps it's just in his nature."

"I know he was in the war. He told me. I suppose he witnessed many awful things, that could explain the darkness."

"And perhaps the kindness, I've heard the stories about men taking care of each other. Perhaps he was some kind of medic or took care of an injured soldier."

"I suppose there are many possibilities. All I know for certain is the war brought out the worst in many men."

Alice shuddered. "I know that only too well."

James turned to her and gestured to her stomach. "And God brought many good things out of the tragedies too."

Alice smiled and placed her hand on the baby. "Yes."

"Good to see you smile about it, Allie. I think you're really beginning to heal."

"I've a long way to go, James."

"I know." He touched her arm. "I'll be here for both of you. You've got friends too. Missy and Clem, and I suppose we can think of Lane as a friend. He seems to genuinely care as you say."

"I suppose so, but I'd rather he didn't know the truth."

"I don't see why he needs to know. Perhaps one day you can tell him, when you're ready."

Alice nodded and gave her brother a shy smile. He pulled the wagon up outside the house and carefully helped her down and up the stairs inside to her room. "Now you get some rest, I'll see to the horses."

Alice smiled, removed her shoes and lay down on the bed, wriggling herself into a comfortable position.

Fourteen

Missy passed Alice a cup of chamomile tea and took the seat opposite her.

"Thank you. It's wonderful to have you home."

"My pleasure. We had a lovely time away but it's good to be back and live here with Clem."

Alice took a sip, looked around and smiled. "You've made this little home so lovely. I'll bet you're happy here."

"Yes. We've only been back a few days, but it feels like we've always lived here."

"I can't imagine living in such a busy hotel with all these people around." Alice gestured to the door that joined their suite to the hotel lobby.

"I find it so interesting, but really we're quite private here. But I won't have a lot of time to spend in the hotel, I start school soon."

"I know. I'm going to miss having you around all the time." Alice sipped at her tea and subconsciously rubbed her stomach.

Missy gripped her friend's arm. "I know. I'll miss you to."

"But the students need you and I'm so glad the town will have a school."

"I'm very nervous. In Craigstown I taught the 6th grade, here I'll be teaching all the grades at once."

"You'll do great, my darling." Clem entered the room with a basket of fire wood, followed by James.

"Thanks for your faith in me." Missy received his kiss and grinned. "Supper's ready." She gestured to the cloth on the table covering the food.

"Wonderful. We'll just wash up." Clem smiled and he and James disappeared through the door toward the washroom.

"That was delicious, Missy, thank you for inviting us." James grinned as he placed down his fork.

"You're most welcome. We hadn't had a chance to have you over since we got back from our honeymoon."

"Oh, we understand, you've been busy." Alice pushed away her plate.

"Yes, but we had to have you over before school starts." Missy stood and began clearing away plates.

"I'll help you with the dishes," Alice offered.

James glared at her.

"James, I'm quite able to help. It won't take long and I'll sit down again afterwards."

Her brother didn't look convinced.

"Truly, I'm not an invalid and I have to be up, doing things sometimes or I'll go mad."

"Alright, just don't overdo it."

"I won't." Alice smiled and put her hands up to Missy.

Missy grinned and helped her friend to stand. Once she was up, she was good to go, it was getting up that proved challenging sometimes.

The men retreated to the living room and sipped at their coffee.

Clem grimaced. "I'm not sure what I'm going to do."

James lowered his cup and frowned. "About what?"

"Owen over at the livery was going to come with me to the city to fetch the new fittings for the restaurant. There are several large items needed including a new stove. I want to go and get them myself as some of the items are very expensive and I don't trust the stage to get them here in one piece. But Owen's daughter has taken ill and they've gone to Clarksfield to take her to the doctor." Clem grimaced again. "I don't suppose you'd come with me? I really do need another man."

James eyed his sister and looked back at Clem. "I'm not sure it's a good idea to leave her."

Clem nodded. "A shame. I could really use your help."

"His help with what?" Alice said as she and Missy joined the men.

"I have to go to the city to collect a number of things still needed for the hotel. I had a man lined up to come with me, but he can't. I was hoping James might accompany me."

Alice sucked her lips under and inhaled sharply.

James gripped her hand. "I couldn't leave Allie alone, especially not over night. We'd be gone a week at least and I'm not sure."

Alice blinked away tears. "I'm sorry that I'm causing so much trouble."

"Hey." James squeezed her hand again. "You are not trouble. I understand why you don't want to be left on your own for too long."

"I'm okay during the day because I know you are at least nearby and so is Clem and Missy, but.... Ohhhhh..."

"I could stay with her."

All eyes swung to Missy. "You'd do that?" Clem asked.

"Yes. I'd rather not be here without you either. I'd be happy for the company. I'll be at school in the day time but at least you could have someone with you in the evenings and over night?"

"I think I could manage that." Alice smiled as confidently as she could.

"Are you sure, Allie? I'm happy to stay if you need me to. I'm sure I can find another man to help Clem."

"I'm sure. It'll be like a sleepover."

Clem turned to Alice. "Only if you're sure."

Alice smiled. "I have to get used to this eventually. I can't live my life in fear."

"Alright, I'll look in on Lane Masters and see if he might check up on you. Would that suit you, Allie?"

Alice nodded. "I think so."

"You said you trust him?"

"I do. But he's never been in our house before." Alice's lip trembled. She prayed for confidence and smiled. "But, I'm sure I'll be alright. God is with me."

"Brave girl." James put his arm around her and kissed her temple. He looked up at Clem. "When do you want to go?"

"The sooner we leave the sooner we can come home. It's a three day ride to Grantville with wagons in tow and we must get there and back before the snows come."

"Well, that could be any day now, we best leave right away." James grimaced. He'd felt the days cooling down and had heard this area was often prone to early storms.

"We'll go first thing tomorrow. Is that alright with you both?"

Both women tried to keep the apprehension off their faces. "Yes." They said in unison and gripped each other's hands.

"You could stay in the boarding house if you prefer?" James suggested.

"No, I'd rather stay at our cabin."

"I'll have the hotel kitchen ladies keep an eye on you. Arthur and the crew can watch the hotel while we are gone. I'm thankful to have competent staff."

James nodded. "Well, I'd best get my sister home, then I'll set about packing my things."

"I'll bring Missy over in the morning, we'll leave around eight?" Clem raised his eyebrows.

"Alright. Do you want me to make breakfast for you both?

James smiled at his sister. "A simple one, something light."

"I'll make us all pancakes they're easy and light."

"Okay then. We'll be over at seven." Clem smiled.

"Very good." Alice smiled.

James drained his cup and stood, reached his hand out to his sister and they left the room to head home before it got too dark.

Clem stood. "I'll just go chat to the hotel staff, fill them in on what is happening."

Missy nodded. "Alright. I'll pack our things."

"Thanks, Sweetheart." Clem kissed her cheek and hurried out the door into the foyer.

* * * *

Lane's head jerked up as the door opened. "Mr. Knight? What brings you to the newspaper at this time in the evening?"

"I'm not here about the newspaper. I wanted to ask you a favor if you don't mind. Mrs. Harvey said I'd find you here."

"Yeah, I wanted to get a head start on tomorrow's issue. What with school starting next week there is a lot to report on."

James nodded. "I understand."

Lane noticed the serious look on Jame's face and stood from his desk. "What is it?"

"I have to go out of town tomorrow. I'm going to Grantville with Clem to collect some things from the hotel..."

Lane smiled and nodded. "I'd be happy to check in on Alice if that's what you're wanting."

James gave him a grateful smile. "Thank you. Missy'll be staying with her while we are gone but I'd be most grateful to have a man around. One that Alice trusts."

"I understand completely. Is she okay with that?"

"Yes. She told me she trusts you." James raised his brows as if he hoped it was true.

Lane walked around the front of the desk and put his hand out to James. "I promise you, I'll look after her with my life."

James gripped his hand and smiled. "Thank you. I wouldn't be able to go if I didn't know there were people looking out for her."

"She's eight months along now, isn't she?"

"Yes. She gets tired so quickly these days."

"That's to be expected. Her body is working hard." Lane stopped himself before he started to sound too much like a doctor.

"Well, I'd best get back to her, she doesn't like to be alone long when it's dark."

"I can understand. When do you leave?"

"Early tomorrow."

"I'll go by everyday, haul wood and make sure she's alright."

"Thank you that gives me a great deal of comfort."

"My pleasure." Lane said as James disappeared out the door. He stood for a moment and scratched his chin, and a wide smile crossed his face. "She trusts me." He squinted into the semi-dark room. "Why does that please me so much?" He'd never felt so drawn to a woman. Not even Emily had tugged at his heart strings like that. Perhaps it was his inner longing resurfacing. Here was a woman in need and his doctor heart was responding. He sighed and spoke aloud as he walked back to his desk. "It's more than that, I don't see her as an unfortunate woman." His lips curled up into a wry smile as he sat back down and picked up his ink pen. "I see her as a beautiful and intriguing woman, who I want to protect." He shook his head at his own sentimentality. He'd never admitted that before but the more he got to know Alice the more he found her beguiling. The more he wanted to wrap her in his arms and keep her safe, to promise her he'd always protect her and the baby. "Always love her," he murmured and smiled to himself.

Recently he'd felt the darkness beginning to lift. The pain in his heart softening. He was even beginning to yearn for medicine again. "Is she the reason?"

Lane put his pen down and smiled. "Just perhaps." He had no idea if she would ever be able to open her heart and really trust a man enough to marry, but that didn't matter to him. He really did just want to see her happy and thriving. Alice and the baby.

"Yes, James, I'll take care of her as though she was my own wife, and the baby was my own." He promised. Unable to concentrate any further he tidied his desk, left the articles out for the morning, picked up his lantern and left the gazette.

For a reason he couldn't place he made his way across to the church, walked up the stairs and strode inside. Heading for the altar he fell to his knees and for the first time in many months he spent time in prayer.

Fifteen

The door slammed behind Missy as she stepped in with an armful of firewood. Alice gasped and turned abruptly. Exhaling loudly, she smiled and the pushed away the threatening fear. "It's awful windy out." She shuddered as the cold gust reached her.

Missy flung the wood in the basket by the fire and hung up her coat. "It's freezing, I'm chilled to the bone." She hurried to the fireplace to warm herself.

"I'll get you some coffee." Alice smiled and soon joined her with two cups. "Why didn't you leave that for Lane? You shouldn't have lingered out there."

"I had to release Candy into the barn anyway, I figured I'd grab an armful in case we need more before supper. Lane'll be by later."

"I'm glad he looks in."

They both took seats in the armchairs before the fire. "How glad?" Missy raised her brows suggestively.

Alice sighed and toyed with her hands in her lap.

"What is it? I was only teasing."

"I know." Alice gave her friend a half smile. "I wish I could think about a future with a man. Lane is a lovely man, and I trust him. He's been kind to me the last three days since James and Clem have been away. If ever there was a man I could think about being it with, it could be someone like him."

"So, what's the problem?"

Large tears filled Alice's eyes. "I don't know if I could ever give myself to him completely. Even though I trust him I'm afraid to let down my guard.

I'm afraid to let myself love. I'm afraid of his touch sometimes."

"Alice, that's to be expected, and it may take time, but I'm confident you'll learn to love. It may not be Lane, but just the fact that you trust him at all is a huge improvement. You aren't afraid to be alone with him." Missy sipped at her cup. "Does his touch remind you of... well... you know."

Alice shook her head and took a sip from her own cup. Holding it in two hands she smiled at Missy. "No. It really doesn't. Lane has touched my arm a few times and has even put his arm around me. I thought it would make me remember, but in a way it makes me forget. Does that make sense?"

Missy nodded. "I think so. Almost like his touch is erasing your memory of what touch used to feel like to you and replacing it with a new memory of how it should feel – loving and gentle."

"That's it exactly."

"Then I have no doubt that one day you'll let a man in. You'll know his embrace is caring and loving and not sinister."

Alice's face became wistful. "I hope so." She rubbed her stomach. "But what about the baby? Do you really think a man could love the baby if they know the truth?"

Missy reached across and gripped her friend's hand. She smiled. "I really do, Alice, and I'm not just saying that."

Alice nodded. It will still take her some time to truly believe it.

Both girls looked at each other in alarm as a gust of wind rattled the windows. "Wow, it's really blowing." Alice grimaced.

Missy jumped up to look out the window. "It's started snowing."

"James said he thought the snow would come soon. I hope it doesn't delay their return."

"It might, but don't worry. I'll stay with you as long as you need me to."

"Thank you, you're a good friend."

"You're welcome. Now come on, want me to help you up so we can make supper?"

"Yes. Thank you." Alice put her hands up to Missy.

*   *   *   *

"Thank you, Lane. We appreciate your help." Missy smiled as he stacked the last armload of wood.

"My pleasure, ladies. Is there anything else you need before I go?"

"No, we'll be just fine." Alice tried to stifle a yawn. Her back had been hurting all day. She longed to be off her feet, but she wouldn't allow herself that luxury until he left.

Lane smiled at Alice's stubbornness. "I'm happy to help, Alice. Really, nothing is a bother."

"I know, and we're grateful to you really, but you go on home, we are all set up here."

"Alright. Promise me you won't go out, the snow is getting deep now, and there are storms across the prairies, so we are bound to get more. I'll come and check on you in the morning, so if you get snowed in don't panic, I'll come to you. You have enough wood to last at least three days, so you certainly won't run out." Lane gestured to the very large pile of wood.

"Thank you." Alice smiled. "I hope the men come back tomorrow. It's been seven days now."

"I know but you mustn't worry, remember their telegram said they have to hold up in Grantsville till the storm eases. They'll be here soon. Don't worry."

"Thank you, again. You're very kind to check in on us. With school closed I'm not getting into town as much." Missy frowned.

"It's my pleasure, and I'll be back in the morning." Lane smiled and touched Alice's arm. "See you tomorrow."

Alice returned his smile, stifling a grimace as a pain shot through her body. "See you tomorrow."

Lane frowned slightly as he caught her wince. "Are you alright? I could camp out in your barn if you need me?"

Alice frowned. "I'm just fine, Lane, don't worry about me."

"If you insist." Lane eyed her, then nodded. He snatched his coat from his hook, and stepped out onto the covered deck, fetched his snowshoes and hurried home, hoping it wouldn't start snowing again until he was back under cover.

Alice let out a slight groan and rubbed her stomach. Missy pivoted on her feet and crossed the room to her. "Are you alright?"

"Yeah. I just need to get off my feet."

"Alright, come on, I'll help you to bed."

Alice wanted to protest that it was still early but she felt sore all over. "Alright." She nodded and let Missy help her to bed.

*   *   *   *

Lane lay awake for some time, his swirling mind keeping him from sleep. Caring for Alice was such a delight to him, almost as if he were looking after his own pregnant wife, except she wasn't his. He longed to be able to hold her and help her through this, to heal from the pain she carried and to give himself to her completely. In loving Alice, his own weary soul was healing.

He'd reconciled with the Lord, he couldn't believe he hadn't done so sooner. Instead of taking his troubles and his burdens to the Lord, he'd buried them deep. If anyone knew the pain of betrayal it was God.

These last few days the nightmares had become less frequent, the pain less consuming and he found himself more hopeful than he'd ever been. Pastor Becroft back in his hometown had once said "It's in loving others that we find the most healing in our own souls." And for the first time he really understood what the pastor had meant.

He could no longer deny that he had feelings for Alice. He worried for her and the baby and prayed for them without ceasing. He petitioned the Lord for her and hoped that one she may come to trust him and love him too.

He sighed loudly and gave up on the idea of any more sleep. It was a little after midnight and the storm had eased. He might as well go and get a head start on the newspaper. That would give him more time during the day to spend watching over Alice. It seemed like James and Clem would be delayed by at least a week by storms across the plains. That was fine by him. He'd watch over the women as long as was needed.

Lane swung his legs over the side of the bed and stood up. He sighed loudly and dressed warmly. Winter had certainly struck early. He didn't bother with his snowshoes as the office was just across the street. He gingerly made his way through the snow all the while praying for the safety of the two women.

Stepping into the office he shuddered as a sudden wind came up bringing with it swirling snow. "Wow!" He exclaimed at his own timing. He struck a match to light the lamp and walked over to the press. Propping up the lantern he went to work setting the type for the middle page of the current edition.

His thoughts continued to swirl as he worked and he prayed this storm wouldn't last long and leave the women trapped in the house.

After some time he stood and stretched his back. Glancing at the clock he grimaced, it was almost four am. He smirked and shrugged. "Might as well keep working the day is nearly beginning." He pressed a row of letters tightly into the plate and carefully checked the type. He snapped his head up as something caught his eye.

He paused and walked to the door. The snow was thick and swirling but he could just make out the flashing of a light. "What on earth?" He grabbed his lantern and walked to the door, pushing it against the snow that was beginning to pile up. He peered out through the snow and howling wind and was dismayed to notice a figure, wrapped tightly in coats, tripping and staggering through the snow with a lantern hanging from its arm. He could barely make out her cries. "help! Please, help."

"What on earth?" He launched himself out into the storm and reached for the woman pulling her back into the Gazette office. The woman was shivering violently and he took the lantern from her. She reached up a shaking hand and pulled down the scarf that wrapped around her nose and mouth.

"Missy?" Fear rolled over Lane. "What is it? Is it Alice? Is everything alright?" He knew she'd never leave Alice if it wasn't urgent.

Missy, shuddered and took a deep breath. "I think it's the baby, she's in so much pain."

Knives stabbed at Lane's heart. "Oh, no." He gripped Missy's arm. "Come with me, you stay at the boarding house, you mustn't go back there in this weather."

"She needs help?"

"I'll go to her. I promise. But it's too dangerous for a woman to be out in this. Come on I'll get you to the boarding house."

She merely nodded, much too disoriented to argue. Lane reached for a blanket that he kept at the office and wrapped it around both of them, carrying the lantern before him they headed out into the storm.

Confident Missy was safe with Mrs. Harvey he headed back out with his snowshoes over his shoulders. He ran next door to the small room marked 'infirmary' and flew inside. Gathering all that he could find he thrust it in a burlap sack. Then, lacing on his snowshoes, he gathered the sack and made his way as fast as he could the half mile through the snow and sleet to the cabin.

"Lord, protect her and the baby, get me there in time to help, and I pray I have what I need. Lord. Please keep her safe. Help me not to get lost in this weather. Amen." At that moment the wind ceased it's howling and the snow slowed some. Lane breathed a grateful prayer and picked up his pace.

He could hear Alice's cries before he reached the front door. "Alice," he called, not stopping to knock, he kicked off his snowshoes and burst inside. "Alice." He called again.

"Help me." Came the pitiful voice and then another loud cry.

Lane hurried toward the bedroom and ran in. "Alice?"

She lay on her bed gripping her abdomen and writhing in pain. "The baby." She managed through gritted teeth.

"It's alright, Alice, I'm here. I'm going to help you."

"I think..." She groaned again. "He's too early."

"Hush, don't worry, trust me. I want to help."

Alice looked at Lane with terror in her eyes.

Lane touched her arm and smiled. He reached his other hand up and brushed some hair back off her face. "Alice, you can trust me. I know what I'm doing."

Alice grimaced, she wanted to protest that they needed a doctor and she wanted James but what was the use. James wasn't there and there was no doctor. She had no choice but to trust Lane. She managed a shaky smile and a nod.

He squeezed her arm. "It's gonna to be alright, I promise." All of a sudden he felt a wave of peace wash over him and the cool calm mind of the doctor returned to him as though it'd never left. "I'm going to examine you." He gave her a confident smile.

His smile and calm manor soothed her a bit and she nodded.

Lane gave her a thorough examination, then washed his hands again and came to her bedside. He took her hand. "Alice, listen to me. Your baby is small but he's not in the right position. You are in labor though. This is going to take a mighty effort, but you can do it. I'll be here with you the whole time."

"I... I don't... I don't think I can."

"Yes, you can. You're strong and brave. You can do this."

Alice looked like she was about to cry so Lane gripped her hand tightly and lifted his other to God. "Lord, I pray for your help and protection..." He had to raise his voice as the storm picked up in fury outside. "Help Alice with this task and keep us all safe in here. Bring this baby into the world and may he be as strong as his beautiful mother." He turned his head and quickly said 'Amen,' hoping his slipped complement hadn't been noticed.

"Thank you." Alice whispered and then cried out as another pain tore through her.

"It's alright. It's going to be alright."

Sixteen

"That's it, Alice, bear down." Lane kept his voice as calm as he could. Alice was utterly exhausted, labor was taking a long time and it required a collossal effort. The baby was small but twisted and she was in much more pain than usual. "Come on, dig deep, Alice, he's almost here."

Alice gripped the sides of the bed as tightly as she could and screamed with all her might, almost drowning out the howling wind with her cry.

"Good, job, ohh, here he comes..." Lane struggled to keep the emotion out of his voice. "That's it, one more big push." He encouraged and she gritted her teeth again and Lane grinned. "ohhh, that's a girl... ohh. Ohhh... It's a girl." He smiled as he assisted the baby into the world. "A beautiful girl." Then his face fell, something was wrong. The baby was twisted and purple and not breathing.

"What... is it?" Alice panted out as she fell back against the bed.

Lane whisked the little girl away and dipped a cloth in the basin to wash her face. He slapped the baby on the bottom but still it didn't breath. Gently he lay her down and began to massage the girl's chest, pressing gently. He leaned down and opened the mouth of the child and cleared out her mouth, turning her over and patting her back, letting the liquid drain. The baby sucked in a raspy breath and its face screwed up tightly in a strained, gasping cry.

Lane breathed a sigh of relief and patted the baby's back a few times, then carefully washed her and wrapped her in a soft blanket.

Alice lay with her head back against the pillow and her eyes closed. Lane approached and gently touched her shoulder. She looked up and smiled.

"Here she is." He passed her the very red-faced baby girl. The little screwed up face continued to whimper.

"She's so tiny." Alice instinctively reached for her and held the bundle against her chest.

"She's premature, and we'll have to be very careful that she doesn't get any infections. Her lungs may not be developed enough to handle it."

Alice squinted at him, but the baby fussed and she patted her back gently. "Is she alright?"

"As far as I know." Lane knew he couldn't keep his past from her for long but for now she hadn't asked.

Alice touched the little face, the baby's eyes were still firmly closed and her lips trembled. She lifted the little girl to her face and kissed the downy head. Then she burst into tears and began to sob, holding the girl close.

Lane pulled up a chair and put a hand on Alice's shoulder as she cried, he wouldn't try to stop her. Her emotions would be all over the place for a time, that was totally normal, and no doubt her circumstances only added to it.

At last, she stopped crying and Lane passed her a handkerchief. "Are you alright."

"Yes, it's just, she's so.... beautiful and I... I just can't help but love her so."

Lane smiled and patted the little girl's back. "I can see why, Alice. She's perfect and I think she looks just like you."

Alice closed her eyes and nodded. "I can't give you up, I love you little girl..." She caught herself before she said more, but Lane didn't ask any questions.

The baby started to cough and wheeze, and Alice looked at Lane with scared eyes.

"Pass her to me."

She hesitated but with a lack of other choices she passed the baby over. Lane placed the baby at the foot of the bed and unwrapped the tight blanket. He hurried to his burlap sack and rummaged through it. Finding a small bottle, he opened it and poured just a drop into the lid.

"What is that?" Alice's eyes were wide with fear as she watched him.

"A little something to loosen up her airways and help her breath." He dipped his finger tip in and rubbed a little inside the baby's mouth and under her nose. The baby continued to wheeze and choke. "Come on, little girl." He encouraged. "Breathe for me."

"Please, don't let her die." Alice placed both hands over her face, overwhelmed with love for the child. "Please, you have to save her."

Lane picked up the nameless baby and began to rock her, patting her back gently. Twice he dipped his finger in the liquid and placed it inside the child's mouth.

"Come on, little girl." He closed his eyes. "Please, Lord." Was all he could manage.

After some time the little girls breathing began to change and her whimpering ceased. Lane breathed a sigh of relief and whispered a grateful prayer. Then the child opened her mouth and began to howl. Alice sat up and her face fell. "What is it?

Lane grinned. "I think she's hungry, that's a good sign, Alice."

"Shall I try to feed her?"

"Yes." He placed the baby down and helped her to sit up the bed as painlessly as possible. "I'm sorry." He said as she winced.

"It's alright."

At last, he had her upright and he reached for the screaming baby and passed her to her mother. He moved across the room to busy himself with tidying up as Alice gingerly opened her blouse. It took some time, but the baby latched on and began to feed.

"Lane."

He turned to look at her, she'd flung a sheet across her to keep her from exposing too much to him. "Yes?" He couldn't help but smile at the absolutely beautiful sight of the mother and baby. The longing in his heart grew stronger.

"How did you know what to do?"

He took a deep breath and exhaled. "I told you, I've been present at births before."

She patted the baby's back. "It's more than that, I've been at a birth before but I wouldn't have known what to do."

"Confession time." He grimaced and flashed her a contrite smile.

She gestured to the seat next to her bed.

He sat down and smiled at her. "Alice, I'm a doctor."

Alice's face fell and she looked at him. "You're a doctor?" *It explains his nurturing nature and why I feel so comfortable with him.*

He nodded.

"Why didn't you tell anyone?"

The baby finished her meal and began to fuss. Lane put his hands out to offer to take her and Alice passed her over. He flicked a towel over his shoulder and gently lifted the tiny baby and began to pat her back. Alice hastily did up her buttons.

The question still hung in the air and as he stood and walked back and forth with the baby, he sighed. "I didn't tell anyone because I thought I'd never be able to go back to medicine."

"But why not, you're obviously very good at it."

"I'll tell you later if you want to know, for now let's just say the war took away any desire I had to pick up a scalpel."

"So, what made you want to help us?" Alice gestured to the baby and they both chuckled as small burps came from the little girl.

Lane passed the baby back to Alice. "I'm not sure. I just felt compelled to help you, perhaps it's God, maybe your circumstances."

"Circumstances?" She bit her lip. Just what did he know?

"You know..." he gestured to her. "You being... a widow and all." He quickly stated.

Alice nodded and yawned loudly.

Lane stood up. "Are you feeling like you might want to rest?"

"Yes. But what about the baby?"

"She'll need careful monitoring, I'll watch her. You take the chance to get some sleep."

"Missy?"

"She's at the boarding house. I don't imagine she'll be back any time soon. Not while this storm rages." He leaned over and touched her arm. "You're quite safe, Alice. Rest. I'll watch the baby."

He lifted the little girl into his arms and bent down again. He stroked Alice's cheek without meaning to. "Sleep."

She turned under her lips, nodded and closed her eyes. Lane took the baby and left the room.

Alice didn't fall asleep right away, her thoughts were much too busy. *Is that why I've always felt safe with him? Because he's a doctor. It makes sense. What was that feeling when he touched my cheek just now? I didn't feel scared or revolted by his touch. In fact it felt loving and thrilling. Perhaps Missy was right.* She smiled and turned her head to the side. *I could never give up my baby. She's so beautiful and perfect. Thank You, Lord.* She barely finished her prayer and fell asleep.

"No... I can't do it... I can't do it." Lane's cries startled Alice awake.

She winced as she climbed out of the bed and walked into the nursery. Lane was asleep on the armchair next to the crib and he was thrashing around. Alice put a hand on his shoulder and shook him. "Lane???"

Lane sat bolt upright and sweat poured from his brow. His fuzzy brain fought to register where he was. He looked up at Alice and grimaced. "Sorry, I'm sorry you had to get up."

"It's alright. Are you alright?"

"Just a dream. I'm sorry." He sighed loudly. "I thought my nightmares were over."

"The war?"

He nodded and began to explain when the baby woke and began to grizzle. "Oh, she's hungry again."

"Maybe she needs changing."

"I'll do it, Alice. You head back to bed, and I'll bring her to you."

"No, I can't stay in bed."

"You've just had a baby..."

"I know, but I want to get up and get on with being..." She smiled as if she couldn't believe her words, "her mother."

"Brave girl." Lane smiled.

"I need to get dressed and clean myself up."

Lane nodded. "Sure. I'll change the baby and check her over to make sure she's alright. I'll bring her to you in the living room."

"Thank you." Alice smiled and hurried to her room. *I can't believe how much I love that little girl.* She got changed and cleaned herself up as fast as she could. *And how much Lane cares.* She looked at herself in the mirror as she did her hair. Her cheeks reddened as she thought about him. *But, no matter how I feel, it doesn't matter, the moment he finds out the truth he'll be horrified. He's a kind doctor is all.* She shuddered as the house shook again. Standing to walk to the living room she smiled at Lane. "This storm doesn't seem to be stopping anytime soon."

She sat in the chair and Lane passed her the baby. He walked toward the window as she unbuttoned her blouse. "Yes I'm afraid we're snowed in."

"Will we be alright?"

"I believe so, we have plenty of wood, as long as the baby stays healthy we shouldn't have a problem. Although I do fear for your reputation with me being here."

"But you're a doctor."

He grimaced. "They don't know that." He gestured toward the town.

"It's alright, my reputation is sullied anyway." She murmured under her breath.

"What do you mean?"

"Oh, ignore me. I don't know what I'm saying?" She left the room to feed the baby.

* * * *

The baby was asleep at last in the cradle by the fire. Lane made pancakes for them both and they sat in the armchairs to eat them. "Sorry, I'm not much of a cook, this is about all I can manage."

"They're fine, but I wish you'd let me cook."

"Alice, you deserve a break, your body has been through some trauma."

She nodded. "It's been a whole day, do you think the baby is out of the woods, now?"

"There have been no more problems with her breathing. I think she's just going to need more care than usual for the first few months. She's still growing."

"We can't keep calling her 'the baby.' I guess I should give her a name."

"There's no hurry. You'll think of a name in time."

They ate in silence and Alice placed down her plate and turned to Lane. "Thank you." Her voice trembled.

"For what?"

"For being here for me. You have been since I arrived in town."

"I'm just doing my job." But he couldn't keep his cheeks from reddening.

"But it wasn't your job, no one knew you were a doctor."

"I guess no matter how hard I tried I can't keep myself from doctoring."

"What kept you from it?"

"Just the horrors of war. I saw things that I'll never forget, Alice. Every day of that horrific war I wished I wasn't a doctor."

"Is that what the nightmare was about?"

He nodded and stroked his stubbly chin. "I've been having them since the war. I tried everything to keep the thoughts at bay but only one thing seems to have made any difference."

"Oh? What's that?"

Lane put his plate on Alice's. "You." He quickly stood up to take the plates to the kitchen.

Alice gasped in a breath.

Lane came back and sat down, he studied his boots.

"Why me?"

He looked up at her and smiled. "Will you allow me to be honest?"

"Yes."

"Ever since I saw you on the train, I haven't been able to get you out of my mind. I never thought I'd see you again but then when you turned up in town... well, let's just say you've been a welcome distraction to my weary heart."

Alice closed her eyes and hung her head.

"Alice?"

"What are you saying?"

"This isn't the right time. There's so much going on here, the baby, the storm..."

Alice smiled. "Lane, we're trapped here for the time being, we might as well talk. Please, I want to know what you mean?"

Lane took a deep breath and exhaled. He smiled. "Alright. I was born and raised on a farm in Virginia. I've wanted to be a doctor all my life. I was so passionate and excited about helping people. I was top of my class at medical school, but I got drafted the day after I graduated.

"Spent two years at various encampments and when I was finally released from the war I fled west, determined to escape and never pick up a scalpel again."

She nodded to encourage him to continue.

"When I saw you on the train it was as though something from outside of me compelled me to help you. And seeing you here, I've found myself drawn to you."

"But why me?"

"I don't know, perhaps God led me to you. All I know Alice is that you've helped me to heal. You and that little darling." He gestured to the crib. "I sat up last night watching her, seeing her tenacity, her strength, her determination to live. She's as brave and beautiful as you are." That time he didn't look away, he fixed his eyes on hers.

Alice's cheeks grew red, and she gave him a shy smile. "Lane. You hardly know me."

"I know that, but I'd surely like to get to know you. The truth is..." He paused and stood and knelt in front of her. "The truth is, Alice, I'm beginning to grow very fond of you."

Alice bit her lip and tears flooded to the corners of her eyes. "Not me. It can't be me."

He lifted a hand to her cheek. "Yes, you."

Her lips trembled and her tears escaped. She couldn't believe how his touch made her feel. She wasn't at all afraid or nervous, or worried he would hurt her. *I can't bare him to know the truth.* She thought to herself as she buried the growing uncertain feelings that washed through her.

"Alice, what is it?" His caring blue eyes searched her face.

"If you knew, you wouldn't feel that way."

"What do you mean? What are you saying?"

Alice stood and brushed past him and stared into the fire.

Lane turned and stood up. "Alice? Whatever it is, it makes no difference to me. I think I'm falling in love with you."

She spun on her heels to look at him, tears washed down her face. "But it's not me you're falling for, not the real me. Just the me I've let you see. If you knew..." She didn't speak anymore, she just buried her face in her hands and sobbed.

Lane dared to take her in his arms, thrilled that she didn't flinch.

Alice felt her heart pounding in her chest as his arms went around her, but it wasn't fear, it was her growing feelings that she could no longer deny.

Lane leaned his cheek on her hair and whispered. "Do you mean because of the attack that left you with child?"

A loud gasp escaped Alice's lips, and she stepped back from him, horror and disbelief etched all over her face. "You know?"

He nodded.

Alice dropped her chin to her chest. "How do you know?" her voice was small and strained.

Lane stepped closer and reached up to lift her chin. "Forgive me, but I overheard your conversation on the train with your brother."

Alice's eyes were filled with tears and her lips shook with her effort at containing the emotion. "You've known all this time?"

He smiled and nodded.

The tears escaped her eyes then and streamed down her cheeks. "Then how could you ever have feelings for me? You know I'm ruined. How could care about the child of that monster..."

He stopped her by placing a hand on her cheek. "Because none of that matters to me."

She lifted sad eyes to him. "Why not? Don't you see me as spoiled?"

He cupped her chin and leaned in and kissed her forehead. "You aren't spoiled, you were hurt by a vile man. But do you know what I see?"

Alice was afraid to know, so she just looked at him and bit her lips tightly together.

He smiled and brushed her cheek with his thumb. "I see a wounded heart that needs cherishing. I see a courageous young woman who has persevered through so much hardship, who's taken a horrible situation and made it beautiful. I see a young mother and a small baby girl who are so in need of a man's tender love and care." He smiled widely and looked her in the eye. "I'd like to be that man."

Alice burst into tears and covered her face with her hands again as she sobbed out all the emotion. Lane took her in his arms again and held her as she shook. Eventually she calmed but she stayed with her cheek against his shirt. "You could really want me?"

Lane smiled and pushed her away from him so he could look at her face. "I do really want you."

Alice closed her eyes and a wide smile crossed her face. She opened her eyes and looked shyly up at him. "I don't know..." she hesitated.

"Listen, I know you're far from healed, I've got a long way to go, too. All I know for certain is I'm falling in love with you, Alice. And I already love that little girl. I want us to be a family some day, when we're both ready. In the meantime, I want to be there for you and for her. I want her to see in me a man that can be trusted. I don't care who conceived her, all I care about is she's part of you."

"And she'll grow up to be a part of you as well." Alice's voice was shy and trusting.

Lane grinned. "Are you saying you want me too?"

"Would it be too forward to admit it?" Her cheeks grew red.

"No way, it thrills me." He cupped her cheek gently. "I promise, no matter how long it takes, I'll always be here for you and for the baby. I'll love you till my dying day, and I will make sure you're safe and protected."

Alice swiped away a tear. "Thank you."

He pulled her into his arms. "You don't have to thank me. Just knowing that you accept me and trust me is more than enough, for now."

"I can't believe someone as wonderful as you could actually love someone as wounded as me."

Lane pushed her back again to look her in the eye. "No more of that. Of course I could love you. And we are both wounded. But with the help of the Lord and this little girl to love, I'm confident we can find the healing we need together."

"I hope so." She blushed and looked up at him. "It's alright if you want to kiss me."

"Are you sure? I don't want to rush you."

"I'm sure. Because your touch isn't sinister like..." Alice stopped herself. "No, that man is getting no more say over my life, no more power in my mind. He no longer exists. All that exists is God, and you and me and.... Alaina." She smiled.

Lane frowned. "Alaina?"

"I figure the baby should have the name of the man who I know will be a wonderful father someday." She blushed deeply, amazed at her own boldness.

Lane's lips began to tremble and he sniffed away the tears that pooled in his eyes. "Do you mean it?"

"Yes. I'm not close to ready to marry yet, this is all so new. But I know I will be, one day, and there is no one else who makes me feel as safe as you do. I admit, I've thought about you. I just thought you could never love me. I think you'll be a wonderful father, and Alaina and me will be in very safe hands."

"Alaina, that's such a pretty name."

"We can call her, Allie or Lainey."

Lane grinned. "She carries the names of both of us. I love that." He brushed her cheek. "Thank you for this wonderful, most precious gift."

"Thank you, for loving me."

Lane leaned in and gently kissed her. "I'll always love you."

Alice felt her heart leap and was overjoyed to know that she could be intimate with him without it terrifying her. She smiled and walked to the crib, lifted out the little girl and kissed her. "Hello, Alaina. I want you to meet, Lane. He's the kindest man I know." She looked up at him shyly again. "I hope he'll be your papa one day."

Lane didn't bother to hide the tears. He reached for the tiny baby and lifted her to his lips. He kissed her hair. "Hello, Alaina, sweet girl. I'll always watch over you and make sure you're safe. I'll always protect you and your beautiful ma."

Alice leaned into him and he wrapped an arm around her, holding the baby between them. They both looked up then and smiled at each other. The storm had ceased.

Seventeen

"Alice!!!" James called as he and Clem leapt down from their horses. Both fetched shovels from the wagon and began to haul snow away from the door as fast as they could. "There's no smoke coming from the chimney."

Missy gasped. "It's been three days. I hope they're alright."

"Lane is with her. I trust him, they'll both be fine." James smiled and yanked on the door, now free from its snowy barrier. He burst inside and looked around as the other two stomped in behind him. All three gasped and then grinned to each other as they observed the scene. Lane sat on the sofa sound asleep. His hand rested on the baby's back as she slept in Alice's arms. Her head in his lap. He'd pulled a blanket up over the two sleeping in his protection.

"Well, that's quite a sight." James raised his brows. "It would seem a lot has happened since we left." He turned to Clem.

Clem and Missy grinned. "I'm so pleased."

Lane startled awake then. "Oh... Ummm." He blushed deeply and grinned sheepishly at them. "Welcome home." He gently touched Alice. "Wake up."

"What is it?" Ohhh." She looked around and sat up abruptly, gently cradling Alaina. She stood up, rather embarrassed to be found in such a position.

Lane stood too, putting his hand on her back in support, he put his hand out to James. "Hello."

"Hello?" James had a rather bemused look on his face.

"James. I can explain..." Alice began.

"Let me." Lane took over. "I came to help Alice, with the baby. You see..." he sighed. "There's something you don't know about me. I'm actually a doctor."

"You are?" James asked.

Clem and Missy gasped. "A doctor?" they said in unison.

James tried to keep the humor from his face. "And this is medicine is it?" He gestured to the two of them.

Lane opted for the direct approach. He put his arm around her waist. "No, James, this is love."

James frowned and crossed his arms.

Alice hung her head, uncertain of what to say.

"I mean it, I'm in love with your sister, and this beautiful little girl." Lane took the baby in his arms and held her so they could see her.

"Ohhhh." Missy gushed. "She's so precious."

James continued to feign his annoyance.

"I want you to know, I plan to wait as long as is needed for your sister. I've been thinking, I'm gonna open a practice here in town. I hope in time, she'll agree to be my wife and we can run the practice together. Sure wouldn't mind being this little girl's Papa." Lane kissed the baby again and squeezed Alice.

Alice held her breath, uncertain what her brother would say.

James stood and stroked his chin. He lowered his head and sighed loudly. Alice began to worry about his response. He looked up at her and a wide grin crossed his face. "Praise Him," he exclaimed and took her in his arms. "I'm so proud of you." He whispered in her ear. "I love you, and I'm so proud of you, Allie, I'm so happy for you."

"Thank you." Was all she could manage.

She stepped back and took the baby from Lane and held her where Missy could see her. They gushed over the little girl.

James and Lane sized each other up. James grinned and put his hand out the Lane. "I'll be proud to call you my brother when the time comes."

"Thank you." Was all Lane could manage.

James spun on his heels then to look at his sister. "Now, may I hold my niece?"

"Yes, of course." Alice passed the baby to her brother.

He held her and cooed. "Allie, she's so beautiful, she looks just like you."

"And she's gonna love her Uncle James." Alice grinned.

"I thought you were going to have a boy." Missy said.

"I hoped it would be a girl." Clem grinned and squeezed his wife.

"Really?" Alice smiled. Lane slipped his arm around her and kissed her hair.

"Yes, just like her lovely mother."

"Thank you, that's most kind." Alice smiled at Clem.

James was absolutely smitten, staring and cooing at the tiny baby. "Is she healthy?" He looked up at Lane.

"Yes, she's a month early and she'll need a little extra care for the first few months, but I'll be here for her as much as I can."

James nodded. "Me too. She's so precious."

"I know, how could I ever have thought I'd not be able to love her." Alice grinned. "I can't help it."

"Well, with all that has happened." James caught himself and grimaced, he glanced at Lane.

"It's alright, James, Lane knows. He's known since the train." She blushed.

James frowned and then smiled. "I'm glad, you couldn't go into it with a lie." He turned to Lane. "Thank you."

"No need, it makes no difference. I just see a beautiful woman and a tiny baby girl in need of love and I'm thrilled to be one to get to love them both."

James swallowed back a lump. "Papa and mama would be pleased, and I'm delighted for you both." He turned back to the baby in his arms. "What's her name?"

"Alaina Bonnie." Alice paused and looked up at Lane.

Missy grinned. "After the man who will be her father one day?"

"Yes, I hope so." Alice gripped Lane's hand. "And will grow up to be just like him."

Missy embraced her friend.

"Alaina Bonnie Cole..." James grinned.

"Knight." Alice smiled. "No more lies. I can't bare it. Soon enough she'll be Masters anyway."

Lane grinned and raised his brows. "Thank you. But I mean it, I'll wait as long as you need me to."

Alice stood up on her toes and kissed him gently. She blushed as she looked around. "Thank you."

James leaned across and kissed Alice's cheek. "I'm so proud of you. And this little girl." He looked back at Lane. "And I'm pleased she'll have another strong and loving man in her life. I'm glad to hear you'll open a practice, this town needs you."

"And I need it. I came here to escape my past and instead I found everything I've ever wanted. Comfort for my weary soul."

Alaina began to cry and James passed her back to Alice. She kissed the little face. "I love you so much baby girl, thank you for bringing healing to my wounded spirit." She looked up. "And all of you."

The End.

About the Author

Jo Dawson grew up on a dairy farm in Wellsford, a small town in the North Island of New Zealand. She spent fifteen years as a teacher in New Zealand and abroad, before becoming a stay-at-home mum and completing her graduate degree in Theology.

She has lived in Australia and the USA for a time, and these experiences have added to her love of people and history. Blessed with a vivid imagination and the love of classical literature and historical fiction, Jo virtually grew up best friends with Anne Shirley, romping with Jo March and her sisters, sailing a raft down the Mississippi with Huckleberry Finn or living in the 'little house' with Laura Ingalls.

Born and raised in a strong Christian family, Jo's faith is at the centre of who she is, with a lifetime of being involved in churches and Christian camps. These two loves, literature and the Lord, have inevitably converged into writing compelling stories of strong Christian women, courageously facing the hardships of life on the frontier. It is her hope that women of all ages would find encouragement from her heroines' experiences that, while fiction, so often mirror even our modern lives.

Jo currently resides in the small North Island town of Waipu in New Zealand, where she lives with her husband, and a very lazy cat.

Other books by J. L. Dawson

Journeys of the Heart Series
Awakening of the Heart
Shepherd of the Heart
Decisions of the Heart
A Home for the Heart
Blessings of the Heart
Legacies of the Heart

Douglas Falls Series
Prequel: The Cost of Duty
A Duty to Love
Twixt Duty and Love
A Duty to Family
The Duty of a Father
A Duty to Serve.

Multiple Author Series (Standalone books).
Hers to Redeem Book 14: Aaron's Anguish
Hers to Redeem Book 18: Mitchell's Misfortune
Hers to Redeem Book 21: Robbie's Roaming
Hers to Redeem Book 22: Rueben's Risk
Winning His Devotion, Book 8: Ezra's Duty
Second Chance Groom Book 9: Romancing the Attorney
Double Trouble Book 10: Jacob's Brides
Double Trouble Book 14: Andy' Brides
Sleigh Ride Book 5: A Sleigh Ride For Aven.
The Matchmaker and the Mother-in-law Book 15: Molly's wedding Dilemma
Wear Hearts and Wounded Spirits Book 11: Hearts at Stake

Standalone Books
To Love Nate – A Companion to Aaron's Anguish.

Where to find these books:
https://www.amazon.com/stores/J-L-Dawson/author
www.jodawsonauthor.com to sign up for my newsletter
jldawsonauthor@yahoo.com to write to the author
Jo Dawson and **J. L. Dawson Author**
-on Instagram and Facebook

Made in the USA
Columbia, SC
13 December 2024

47928320R00102